KT-143-339

BEACON STREET GIRLS

This book belongs to:

Milly Logan-Wilson
13

VERITAS AMICITIA GAUDIUM
truth friendship fun!

™

Be sure to read all of our books:

BSG Special Adventure Books:

Coming soon:

Time's Up

BY
ANNIE BRYANT

ALADDIN MIX
NEW YORK   LONDON   TORONTO   SYDNEY

This book is a work of fiction. Any references to historical events, real people, or real locales are used fictitiously. Other names, characters, places, and incidents are the product of the author's imagination, and any resemblance to actual events or locales or persons, living or dead, is entirely coincidental.

ALADDIN MIX

Simon & Schuster Children's Publishing Division

1230 Avenue of the Americas, New York, NY 10020

Copyright © 2008 by B*tween Productions, Inc.,

home of the Beacon Street Girls.

Beacon Street Girls, KGirl, B*tween Productions, B*Street, and the characters Maeve, Avery, Charlotte, Isabel, Katani, Marty, Nick, Anna, Joline, and Happy Lucky Thingy are registered trademarks of B*tween Productions, Inc.

Illustrations copyright © 2008 by Pamela M. Esty

All rights reserved, including the right of reproduction in whole or in part in any form.

ALADDIN PAPERBACKS, ALADDIN MIX, and related logo are registered trademarks of Simon & Schuster, Inc.

Designed by Dina Barsky

The text of this book was set in Palatino Linotype.

Manufactured in the United States of America

First Aladdin MIX edition June 2008

4 6 8 10 9 7 5

Library of Congress Control Number 2008920654

ISBN-13: 978-1-4169-6422-3

ISBN-10: 1-4169-6422-3

1010 MTN

Who's Who

BSG

Katani Summers
a.k.a. Kgirl . . . Katani has a strong fashion sense and business savvy. She is stylish, loyal & cool.

Avery Madden
Avery is passionate about all sports and animal rights. She is energetic, optimistic & outspoken.

Charlotte Ramsey
A self-acknowledged "klutz" and an aspiring writer, Charlotte is all too familiar with being the new kid in town. She is intelligent, worldly & curious.

Isabel Martinez
Her ambition is to be an artist. She was the last to join the Beacon Street Girls. She is artistic, sensitive & kind.

Maeve Kaplan-Taylor
Maeve wants to be a movie star. Bubbly and upbeat, she wears her heart on her sleeve. She is entertaining, friendly & fun.

Ms. Razzberry Pink
The stylishly pink proprietor of the Think Pink! boutique is chic, gracious & charming.

Marty
The adopted best dog friend of the Beacon Street Girls is feisty, cuddly & suave.

Happy Lucky Thingy and alter ego Mad Nasty Thingy
Marty's favorite chew toy, it is known to reveal its alter ego when shaken too roughly. He is most often happy.

more on beaconstreetgirls.com

Part One
Kgirl Enterprises

1

Rock Steady

T hey have harnesses and stuff, right?" Maeve asked in a tremulous voice. "I mean, to catch you if you fall off?"

At the words "fall off," Katani swallowed hard. She too felt nervous at the sight of the ginormous, gray climbing wall. *I can't believe I'm actually going to climb it,* she thought. But she reached down and gave Maeve's clammy hand a reassuring squeeze. "Chillax, girlfriend. Look at Avery. She can't fall." Sure enough, Avery, the most athletic of the group of friends, was already securely harnessed and had started her climb.

Katani tried to distract herself from her fears of looking like a total spaz on the wall by concentrating on her favorite magazine, *T-Biz! A Magazine for Teen Entrepreneurs.* As she flipped another page with her free hand, a colorful ad suddenly caught her eye. "This is incredible!" she blurted out loud, before she could stop herself.

"Whoa! That's the spirit, Katani!" Avery shouted encouragingly, giving the Kgirl a thumbs-up as she dangled in her harness.

Katani looked up, slightly embarrassed by her outburst but glowing with excitement about what she had read. "No, no, it's not that, Ave. Forget the wall. It's this contest—an 'Entrepreneur of the Year' contest for middle-school students! Listen . . ." But Avery was already facing the wall and the pint-size climber hadn't heard a word she had said. Katani figured Avery was probably too busy trying to beat the boy next to her up the wall.

"You better put that magazine away, Miss Fashion Biz, and listen to the instructor, or you'll be hanging every which way when it's your turn," warned a suddenly serious Maeve, her big blue eyes glued to the climbers scrambling up the wall like little spider people. Maeve gasped as one climber slipped and fell away from the wall.

But Katani couldn't care less about the rock climbers. In fact, she wished she had stayed home. *T-Biz!* was seeking "the next generation of business leaders." This was *so* up her alley. Kgirl Enterprises was her ultimate fantasy. She should be home now writing up her "detailed, viable business plan" instead of climbing like a giant bug up some *craaazy* wall. Why had she agreed to come? The contest offered "an opportunity for all young entrepreneurs to fulfill their dreams." Katani looked around to see if she could find a quiet place to keep reading.

A sudden blur on the rock wall grabbed her attention. "That girl just fell ten feet!" she yelped.

Maeve, who had been waving for Charlotte and Isabel to come over, spun around. The little girl was now hanging in midair. Maeve's legs began to tremble.

"She's fine," a boy standing behind the girls said.

Maeve turned around to see two of their friends from school. "Hey! Dillon and Nick! What are you doing here?"

"How can Isabel just stand over there and draw?" Katani commented, glancing over at Isabel, who was intently sketching one of the climbers. "My hands are shaking so much, I don't think I could hold a pencil!" she said as she quickly zipped her magazine in the pocket of her sweatshirt. While she liked Dillon and Nick, no way was she ready to share that she was going to enter the *T-Biz!* entrepreneur contest with the two most popular boys at Abigail Adams Junior High. Dillon could be a big tease, and she didn't want to be his latest target. She could just hear him in the cafeteria announcing, "Katani's going to be on the next *Oprah*. Uh-huh!"

"What are *we* doing here? What are *you* doing here?" The good-looking Dillon pointed at Maeve's hot pink yoga pants. He had a low tolerance for all that pink girly stuff. "Nice climbing gear, Maeve," he teased.

She punched him in the arm.

"Seriously, I didn't know you Beacon Street Girls were rock girls," Nick Montoya joked, his eyes on Charlotte, who had just reached the group. "We've been climbing for months," he added proudly.

"This is my first time," Katani offered. She totally didn't want the guys thinking she was any kind of expert. Especially since she was now convinced that she would be slip sliding down that wall any minute now.

"We're forming a team so we can compete. Rock climbing is, like, the coolest sport ever. Hey, check out the Ave." Dillon pointed to Avery grabbing the top of the wall. "Leave it to Avery to beat an experienced climber like Josh on her first try." He shook his head in admiration.

"Well, it's not really Avery's first time. She's tried it a couple of times in Colorado," Charlotte piped up. Then she blushed, thinking that maybe she sounded like she was putting Avery down. She was, in fact, really proud of her friend and just wanted to explain that Avery was pretty skilled already.

"Well, Avery definitely should join our team, then. We're going to need all the help we can get because we aren't that great," Nick said, laughing.

"Hey! Speak for yourself, dude," Dillon protested. Charlotte and Katani looked at each other. They both knew what the other was thinking: Why weren't more boys like Nick Montoya. He wasn't braggy and show-offy like most of the boys they knew.

Suddenly, Avery was in front of them. "A team? I want to join a team! I'm in, right, guys?"

"Oh, yeah!" Nick said.

"Sweet!" Avery threw her fists in the air. "Okay, guys. We gotta find some supercompetitive climbers if we want to win. Let's get together. . . ."

Avery was interrupted by Chris, the muscled instructor, who faced the group. "Okay, ready to rock steady, ladies?" He pointed at the wall behind them. Katani stared at the huge structure, and Maeve made a funny scaredy-cat face. The wall towered over them, looking impossibly high.

Katani felt her stomach twist into knots just looking at it. She glanced over at Maeve, who was tapping her right foot up and down while clasping and unclasping her hands together. Katani stifled a nervous giggle. Competitive friends, a looming contest deadline, and now another opportunity to demonstrate her total *lack* of athletic skills? That was just too many walls to climb!

"Chill out, guys! We'll catch you after your lesson." Dillon waved as he and Nick exchanged a laughing look and walked away from the girls.

"I'll give it another go." Avery grinned, turning her full attention to Chris.

"Where's Isabel?" Charlotte suddenly looked concerned. Katani and Maeve glanced around the crowded gym but couldn't see their dark-haired friend anywhere. "You girls have to get going or we're going to run out of time," an impatient Chris warned them. "I've got another lesson coming up," he explained.

The BSG turned their heads to face him when suddenly Isabel appeared out of nowhere, clutching her notebook. She popped in line next to Avery. Katani whispered, "You better stash that sketchbook in your backpack or it will get lost." Isabel's eyes widened. Her sketchbook was too important to her to ever let it get lost.

"Excuse me, Mr. Instructor." Isabel waved her hand. Maeve couldn't help giggling. "What?" Isabel stared at her friend. "I just want to know if I can go and put my notebook in my backpack. There may be great works of art in here." The artist of the group grinned.

Chris just shook his head. "Hurry up," he said, squelching a smile. He began counting as Maeve started a little impromptu hip-hop routine to one, two, three and Isabel sprinted across the gym, darting in between climbers and parents. Stashing her sketchbook in her green backpack, she was back in less than twelve seconds. Avery gave her a high five and the BSG were ready to climb . . . well, three of them were. Linking pinkies, Katani nibbled on her lip and Maeve twirled a curl.

Chris carefully went over the general climbing rules again and showed the girls how to strap on the safety ropes. Within minutes, all the BSG were harnessed and on the beginners' wall. A couple of experienced climbers came over to belay them.

"You're doing great, girls. Go at your own pace, hold by

hold," Chris called up to them as they began to inch up the wall.

Avery scaled half the wall in seconds, then stopped to look down at her friends. "Go, BSG! You definitely have the hang of it."

"We better have the 'hang' of it," Charlotte said with a laugh, gripping the colorful ridges of rocks on the wall with her fingers and toes, "or we're in trouble!"

"I'm going to demolish this wall!" Avery announced, scrambling like a mad monkey to the top.

"Look at us, we're really doing it!" Isabel yelled up to the triumphant Avery.

Avery hung at the top while Isabel and Charlotte kept a steady though slow pace. "Rock it," she shouted down to her friends, but couldn't help glancing at the overhang on the twenty-foot route next to her. She would be climbing that within a month, she promised herself as she zipped back down the wall with her usual natural athletic abandon.

"Nice work up there," Chris told her.

"Thanks. Can I try the intermediate wall?" Avery jogged in place, trying to be patient, but about to jump out of her skin. She wanted a bigger challenge than the beginners' wall.

"I see you're ready to go, but let's give your other friends a minute to catch up."

Avery looked up. She couldn't believe what she was seeing. Despite her long limbs, Katani had made it only a few yards up the wall and looked as scared as if she were climbing Mount Everest instead of a beginners' wall. Avery had to cover her mouth to keep from laughing out loud. Katani must have seen Avery watching because she suddenly flung herself back to the wall with her determined Kgirl look.

Katani actually managed to scramble up about a foot. *Not*

too bad for an unathletic beginner! Katani thought as she gave herself an imaginary pat on the back.

Suddenly a screaming, flailing Maeve flew out from the wall sideways. Avery couldn't hold it in any longer—she burst into a humongous belly laugh. With her hair flying and her bright pink pants flapping, Maeve looked like a wild and crazy flamingo. She must have flown out a good five feet from the wall before she was saved by the safety harness.

"Hey look, Maeve's auditioning for *Fear Factor!*" Avery yelled a little louder than she intended. Everybody in the gym turned to look.

Though Maeve seemed more than slightly terrified, she just couldn't stop her performer self from taking over. She pushed herself off the wall again, flung her arm out, and bent her leg. She shouted, "Not *Fear Factor*, *Peter Pan*—the next time it comes to Broadway!"

Half the people in the gym were staring up at her. Dillon was laughing so hard he could barely stand up. A small, scared smile spread across Maeve's face, and still she was such a ham! Avery swore Maeve would do anything for attention.

Finally, an embarrassed but radiant Maeve was lowered to the ground, where she took a sweeping bow. A minute later, Katani joined her, looking like she had just run the Boston Marathon. "I think I'll stick to horseback riding," she said, wiping the sweat off her forehead.

"I guess I'm not going to make your rock-climbing team," Maeve said, smiling sweetly at Dillon.

"You'll have to start your own team with Tinkerbell and Wendy," Dillon told her.

"Yeah, in Neverland," Nick added.

"Maeve, you crack me up!" Avery was trying to swallow her laughter. "I'm so glad you came. I bet I could learn to climb every wall in here, but I could never create the scene you just did!"

"Only Maeve," Dillon agreed.

Nick was watching Charlotte and Isabel descending. "You did great!" he yelled to them as they landed.

"Everything okay here?" Muscle Man stood in front of them, dwarfing Dillon and Nick.

"Fine, thanks," Maeve said, with an innocent expression as she flung her red curls over her shoulder with a flourish. "I guess the stars indicate that I belong on the ground."

"Have to say, we don't get to see rock climbing like that every day. Hope to see you girls again," Chris said, then turned back to the wall.

The BSG clasped arms and dashed for the locker room. Life on the wall had rocked their day.

2

Big Dreams

$\mathcal{A}$s cool as it was hanging out at the rock gym with her friends all afternoon, Katani was anxious to get started on her business plan. Running her own company was her big dream, and entering this contest was a great way to start. As soon as her homework was done, she curled up at the foot of her bed to brainstorm ideas. She brought out her new notebook, the one in her signature sunflower yellow color, decorated with tiny white polka dots around the border. Perfect for inspiration! She grabbed her favorite green highlighting pen and began.

"Right." She sighed out loud as she carefully read the rest of the information. "*T-Biz!* promotes creativity among youth and helps young entrepreneurs make connections to benefit their communities by making community service a required component of the competition—" and so on and so on. Her eyes nearly popped out of her head when she read that "Ten winners from across the country will go to Washington, D.C., to meet the heads of Fortune 500 companies." *My life is about to explode!* An over-the-top Katani could barely contain her excitement. She imagined herself walking up to the podium amidst loud clapping and thanking her friends and family for all their wonderful support.

Suddenly her alarm buzzed—the signal to get her clothes and backpack in order for tomorrow. But her prep would have to wait. Katani wanted to finish reading about the contest. When she scanned down the form to the application deadline, her face dropped. *Next Saturday!* Could she really pull all of this together in a little over a week? *Of course she could do it.* Hadn't her friends said she was the most organized of all the BSG? Even more than Charlotte, who had traveled all over the world. Katani decided she would start with the most important thing in any plan:

The Kgirl list.

Kgirl™ To Do:

1. Fill out application— make copies.
2. Recommendations from a teacher (ask Grandma Ruby)
3. Take photos of product (ask Chelsea Briggs?).
4. Sales plan and figures
5. Promotion plan
6. Detailed budget
7. Community service aspect???

Satisfied, she put down her pencil. *All good things start with a list*, she thought, and smiled. The contest deadline *was* super tight, but her confidence was growing. Hadn't she been thinking about the Kgirl Fashion and Advice Empire for years? *Piece of cake*, she told herself.

Katani's heart beat faster when she thought of surprising her entire family with the news that she'd won the contest. They would be so proud of her, and she'd have done it all on her own! Katani figured that she should share her plans only with the BSG to keep the secret. Of course she'd have to include Grandma Ruby, too, since she'd be asking her grandmother, the principal of Abigail Adams, to write a recommendation. Well, maybe she wouldn't tell Grandma Ruby until right before the deadline and then she'd swear her to secrecy—she didn't want to ruin the surprise. But now she had to think of a business plan and get it going immediately.

Her eyes drifted across the room, over her desk with its stacked blue, labeled trays, magazine holders, and pencil holders, to her sewing corner where she tucked her sewing and knitting materials behind a folding screen. Somehow a half-finished scarf had fallen off the back of her sewing chair, and the sky blue mohair yarn had rolled across the floor.

Then it hit her. Her scarves! Everyone loved her scarves—even Avery, who never saw anything interesting in clothes. She said that Katani's scarves were totally unique—signature Kgirl. Selling handmade scarves to friends and family would be the perfect business idea. All she had to do was figure out a way to tie them into some bigger idea, some kind of community service. *Piece of cake*, she told herself again.

Ignoring a sudden flip-flop of her stomach, she jumped

off the end of her bed and reached into the closet for her bathrobe and slippers. At that moment, Katani's sister Kelley marched in with Mr. Bear tucked under her arm. Although Kelley was older than Katani, her autism meant that she sometimes acted like a younger sister. Kelley never went anywhere without her stuffed bear. Tattered and worn, the ratty bear was Kelley's constant companion. Bypassing her own messy bed, Kelley made a beeline for Katani's, flopped next to the open *T-Biz!*, and began reading.

"Mr. Bear likes to read." Kelley propped Mr. Bear over the contest so he could read the rules too. "Look, Mr. Bear. A contest—I'm going to make clothes for you."

"Did you see my other slipper anywhere?" Katani asked from the closet. She wanted to distract her sister from the contest or Kelley would bother her all night about it.

"We can do it! Yes, we can. Mr. Bear and I can do it. We can make some beary, beary nice bear clothes." She laughed out loud at her own joke.

Katani marched over to Kelley's bed and lifted her sister's comforter to find a row of shoes and slippers, including hers, each filled with a stuffed animal and Kleenex or some sort of treasure. Katani dumped some shiny yellow coins and a blue bearded troll glued with glitter out of her slipper. *Don't yell*, she told herself. *Don't say a thing!*

"Did you hear me, Katani? Mr. Bear and I are going to enter the contest too."

"That's cool, Kel," Katani said, trying to keep her voice level, and left the room as nonchalantly as she could. She loved Kelley a lot, but sometimes her sister could be so annoying. She just hoped Kelley didn't reveal her plans to anyone.

Chat Room: BSG

File Edit People View Help

4kicks: we rocked 2day, esp. Maeve! what a total ham!
lafrida: so tru. i loved it, but I think Maeve had the best time
4kicks: i thought dillon was going 2 die he was laughing so hard
skywriter: katani seemed more embarrassed than maeve
4kicks: id bet a lot of $ neither 1 shows at watertown rock adventure again
skywriter: They were trying hard but climbing is def not their thing
4kicks: so who is on for the team
skywriter: big time GROAN. i really want 2 join the team but theres so much going on
4kicks: dont tell me u r going to wimp out ?
skywriter: i dont want 2 but im kinda worried about the big english paper ms r said would b due soon
4kicks: WHAT paper?
skywriter: remember ms r

7 people here

4kicks
lafrida
skywriter
DJsoxfan
montoya33
flikchic
Kgirl

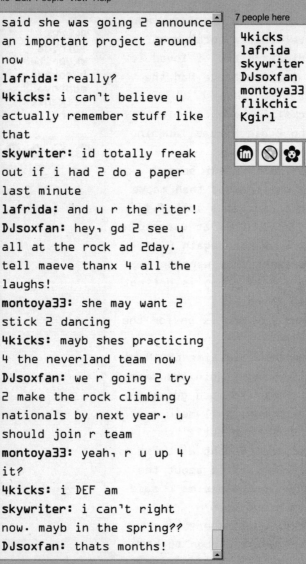

said she was going 2 announce
an important project around
now

lafrida: really?

4kicks: i can't believe u
actually remember stuff like
that

skywriter: id totally freak
out if i had 2 do a paper
last minute

lafrida: and u r the riter!

DJsoxfan: hey, gd 2 see u
all at the rock ad 2day.
tell maeve thanx 4 all the
laughs!

montoya33: she may want 2
stick 2 dancing

4kicks: mayb shes practicing
4 the neverland team now

DJsoxfan: we r going 2 try
2 make the rock climbing
nationals by next year. u
should join r team

montoya33: yeah, r u up 4
it?

4kicks: i DEF am

skywriter: i can't right
now. mayb in the spring??

DJsoxfan: thats months!

7 people here

4kicks
lafrida
skywriter
DJsoxfan
montoya33
flikchic
Kgirl

montoya33: i hear u. btween school and work climbing takes all my extra time. wat about u, Isabel?

lafrida: i wish :) but my Mom says Im way too busy now

montoya33: i have 2 go. my mom has a new pastry she wants me 2 sample

4kicks: does she need other volunteers?

montoya33: ill bring 1 2 school monday! c u

DJsoxfan: check u later bsg

flikchic: So what were u reading at the gym Katani

skywriter: hey maevelicious . . . Kgirl

Kgirl: 0k I need a pinkie swear here

4kicks: you got it

skywriter: absotively

lafrida: totally

flikchic: u can trust us

Kgirl: im going to enter a contest for young entrepreneurs in T-Biz magazine

4kicks: that's cool but why don't u want anyone to know

7 people here

4kicks
lafrida
skywriter
DJsoxfan
montoya33
flikchic
Kgirl

Kgirl: cuz I want to win. dont want a lot of competition

lafrida: we could help u . . .

skywriter: yeah. I'm in

4kicks: I got it—how bout we do a dog walking biz—marty could be the mascot

Kgirl: wait a minute I want this to be mine Im the one who is interested in business not u all . . . gotta go.

7 people here

4kicks
lafrida
skywriter
DJsoxfan
montoya33
flikchic
Kgirl

Katani closed *T-Biz!* and slid it under her bed. She hated the idea of competing with her friends. It made her feel weird inside, like maybe she couldn't trust her friends. She wondered whether she should have told them anything about this project at all. *Wait just a crazy minute!* The BSG were her best friends in the whole world and she needed their help if she was going to make the contest deadline. Confused, she lay back on her bed, turned out her light, and was about to drift off to sleep when she felt something tickling her nose. Kelley had put a little blue feather on her pillow.

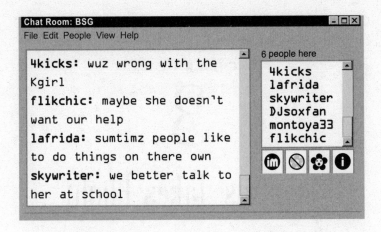

Avery's Blog:

Awesome news! I'm going to join the Watertown Adventure Climbing Team! This totally rocks (haha). We're going to shoot for the nationals next year. If you have a rock-climbing story, post a comment.

I know I'm piling it on this week (including a whopping English project I just found out about). We have an AAJH exhibition game against Palmer on Thursday night at the TD Banknorth Garden. So if you're not into rock climbing, at least buy tix for the Celtics that night to cheer us on!

That's all for now.

P.S. Mom doesn't know about the English assignment or she probably wouldn't have let me join the team. So ixnay on saying anything about it when she's around, okay? I'll tell her soon.

CHAPTER

3

Pegasus Takes Flight

On Sunday the air was crisp and crystal clear. *A perfect day for riding,* thought Katani as she leaned back against her seat. Grandma Ruby steered Triple B, her big blue Buick, up the long driveway as Katani watched the sun glinting off the scaffolding surrounding the barn. By next spring, High Hopes would be renovated and painted, with the outdoor ring cleared and ready for riding. All the old fences would be replaced and painted white and the paddocks would be replanted with luscious green grass. Katani smiled. She imagined her horse, Penelope, grazing in this future pastoral scene as Grandma Ruby pulled into the parking area.

Kelley leaned toward the car door, ready to leap out. "Wilbur, Wilbur, Wilbur," she sang with a carrot in hand.

"Hold your horses, hon," Grandma Ruby said. "We're almost there."

"Bad horse joke, Grandma," said Kelley with her arms folded across her chest.

"Remember the first day we came and we couldn't stand the smell?" Katani laughed as she rolled down the window.

"Smelly horsey smell," Kelley said. "Yum. I want to smell Wilbur all day. He smells so soft and gray."

"I always wanted to ride when I was a girl. I'm so very happy I get to watch my granddaughters do it now." Grandma Ruby shifted into park, and the girls jumped out and raced to the barn.

"Slow down, Kelley! You don't want to spook the horses, now, do you?" Claudia McClelland, the riding instructor, called after Kelley, who was racing toward Wilbur's stall. Eyes wide, Kelley slowed down and tiptoed exaggeratedly through the barn. Katani clapped her hands over her mouth, trying to suppress a giggle. Sometimes Kelley was just too darn funny.

A tall, chestnut quarterhorse with just a snip of white on her nose poked her head through her stall door. Penelope flicked her ears in Katani's direction. Katani rubbed her cheek against the horse and scratched behind the mare's ears.

"Hi, pretty girl. I missed you," she whispered gently as Penelope pushed her nose into Katani's coat. "I know what you want."

Katani put the apple flat on her palm, and Penelope munched it in two bites. Then Katani led the big horse to the cross-ties, where she groomed and saddled her. At the other end of the barn, Katani could see Samantha, one of the stable hands, throwing the bucket saddle on Wilbur while Kelley carefully brushed the small gray horse's mane over and over, all the while singing to him.

Katani waited for Catherine, the other stable hand, to check her saddle. Sometimes Penelope bloated out her stomach too much when Katani tightened the girth.

"You got it right today. Good job!" Catherine complimented Katani as she held the reins over Penelope's head while Katani slipped the snaffle bit in. Katani never ever would have imagined herself doing this a few months ago. She held the reins together near the bit with her right hand and grabbed them with her left hand to make sure they didn't dangle.

Then she led Penelope toward the ring, right behind Whitney Bainbridge's enormous bay gelding, almost a hand taller than Penelope. Whitney, who was the best rider in the class, wore slick tan riding pants with a padding of suede on the inside calves, a goosedown vest over a black turtleneck sweater, and leather boots the same color as her brown velvet hard hat. Her shiny brown ponytail swished across her back.

Katani looked down at her own plain black paddock boots. *Thank goodness I polished these last night,* she thought. She was proud that she'd paid for the boots herself—and she was pretty sure that Whitney never had to pay for anything. How could any girl her age afford to buy riding clothes that expensive?

Penelope whinnied as Katani led the mare toward their class. Suddenly, Katani felt an irrepressible urge to do something—*anything*—to impress Whitney Bainbridge. She hadn't planned on saying anything about the contest to her riding friends, but when they reached the ring, she blurted, "So yesterday I heard about this young entrepreneur contest. It sounds totally cool. You just have to write up a business plan and budget, and if you win, you get to go to Washington, D.C., to meet with the heads of all these huge companies." She felt good showing Whitney that she was a go-getter, too.

"That sounds awesome," said Marky.

"It sounds like a whole lot of work," commented Ling.

"I don't even know what business I'd try!" Marky laughed. "What are you going to do, Katani?"

"I think I'm going to knit scarves. But I still have to figure out how to tie my plan into the community service that's part of the project." She glanced up at Whitney, whose blue-gray eyes were like ice looking at her.

"When's the deadline?" Ling asked.

"That's the scary thing," Katani told them. "It's just one week away."

"That's crazy," Whitney said coolly, slipping on a pair of leather gloves with suede reinforcements on the palms and fingertips. "There's no possible way that someone can pull a business together that fast, unless you have a couple of experienced helpers."

"I'm going to do this by myself," Katani responded in an annoyed tone. Whitney might be able to buy anything she wanted, thought Katani as she looked again at Whitney's beautiful calfskin gloves, but what did that girl know about business, anyway? From the looks of it, Whitney had everything handed to her on a silver platter.

"I could help you." Whitney looked up sharply at Katani.

Whoa, back up, Katani thought. Why would this girl want to help? Besides, she didn't trust Whitney one bit. There was something about her that reminded Katani of Anna and Joline, the Queens of Mean at Abigail Adams. If the QOM were nice, it was only because they wanted something, or to get a good laugh. Their business was to make others feel bad in order to feel good about themselves.

"Well . . . I've been thinking about my business for a long time," Katani finally managed to say, turning away from Whitney to stroke Penelope. "I'm used to working alone."

"All right, riders, let's mount and walk around the ring," Claudia called out, swishing a crop in the air.

Katani turned her focus back to riding. As soon as she sat tall in the saddle with her head held high, she felt the tension leaving her body and relaxed into the rhythmic motion of Penelope's gait. Penelope's ears flicked back as Katani spoke softly, "Good horse. Today we're going to jump. Are you ready, girl?"

Penelope was raring to go. Two weeks ago they had walked and trotted over ground poles. This week they'd try a low jump.

After a quick warm-up, Claudia said, "Okay, jumpers, raise your stirrups two holes." She pointed her crop and said, "Eyes straight ahead, Marky. Ling, you're leaning forward too much. Whitney, why don't you go first, then Katani and everyone else follow in the order you're in."

Katani's heart was pounding, even though the cross-rails set up in the middle of the ring were only a foot high. She went over in her head what Claudia had told them at the last lesson: "Remember, when you get to the jump, lift your weight forward and slide your hands up to the crest of your horse. Let your horse stretch until he's over."

"Okay, go for it, Whitney," Claudia said. "Check your leads," she instructed everyone.

Whitney sailed over in beautiful form. How could Katani ever do it that well? She'd completely die of embarrassment if she fell off in front of Whitney.

"Next," Claudia called.

As they rounded the corner, Katani pressed her heels into Penelope's side and clucked, so Penelope broke into a fast trot, then a slow canter. Katani counted the strides as they approached the first jump. Just before the jump, when she felt Penelope ready to leap forward, Katani slid her hands half-way up Penelope's neck, grabbed a clump of mane, and sunk her weight into her heels. She felt like she was on Pegasus, soaring through the air. It was magical. Horse and rider landed smoothly, and Katani sat back, letting the reins slide through her fingers.

"Nice work, Katani. Next."

Katani's heart soared as she slowed Penelope to a trot and patted her and told her what a good girl she was. She wished everyone from gym class at school could see her now. Mr. McCarthy always expected her to be good at basketball, as if she'd just start playing like her star sisters one day. That was never going to happen. She was an uncoordinated mess on the basketball court. It was hard to believe she was even related to Candice and Patrice. But riding was different. She and Penelope understood each other. Confident, Katani sat up straighter and posted around the ring. Next lesson, she and Penelope would jump even higher.

Three Hundred Dollars

Claudia walked over as Katani was dismounting. "You did a nice job out there today, Katani. Why don't you and Kelley sign up for Pony Camp this summer? But you better do it fast because the slots fill quickly."

"I'll talk to my parents," Katani replied eagerly as she grabbed the reins under Penelope's head.

"The applications are in the office. Grab one before you leave today."

"Thanks, Claudia."

Excited, Katani led Penelope back to the cross-ties, where she started to rub and brush down the pretty mare. She would absolutely love to go to Pony Camp. A whole week with a horse of her own to take care of—how cool would that be?!

Out of the corner of her eye, Katani saw Whitney wiping

down her bay in quick, efficient strokes. Whitney was as tall as Katani and though she didn't wear makeup, there was something perfect about her face, like a doll's. Her eyebrows looked like they'd been waxed into neat arcs, her nose was small and buttonish, and her lips were heart-shaped. *She could easily be a model*, Katani thought, and made herself look away.

"Katani?" Samantha asked.

Katani looked up, startled.

"You won't forget to clean Penelope's hooves, will you?"

"No. No, I won't. I promise," Katani said, embarrassed that she *had* forgotten.

She immediately retrieved the pick and started with the front hoof. She clucked and squeezed the back of Penelope's lower leg until the horse gently lifted her foot, which Katani placed in the palm of her left hand. With her other hand, she dug out the dirt and muck stuck in the soft leathery pad.

Katani looked up to see that Whitney was rubbing Penelope's nose. A piece of paper was in one hand. At the top it read "Pony Camp." Of course she was going, too, Katani thought. She was the best rider at High Hopes, and money wouldn't be an issue.

"So, Katani," Whitney started. "I know you have a lot of ideas already, but I could help you with your business plan. I've done this sort of thing before."

"Okay, thanks. I'll let you know if I need help." *Why won't this girl just drop it already?* Katani thought with irritation. *Maybe Whitney's a stalker*, she thought unkindly.

Whitney folded the Pony Camp application into squares and slid it into her vest pocket. Then she lifted her velvet-trimmed hat and unclipped a barrette from her golden brown hair. "I make these. I paint them all. It's my 'business.'"

Tiny brown horses with blue ribbons strewn in their manes and tails pranced at either end of the barrette Whitney held out. Katani had to admit they were much nicer than any of the painted barrettes she'd seen in JB's Bead, Yarn, and Craft store. She reminded herself to tell Isabel about them, since she was always looking for new arty ideas.

"I sell them at horse shows. I made three hundred dollars last month at the big show at Myopia."

"Three hundred?" Katani was impressed in spite of herself. She'd made only one hundred dollars total from Kgirl Enterprises so far. She was shocked someone her age could make that much money.

"I'm going to be selling these at Dover Saddlery as soon as I get enough of them painted," Whitney informed her with a toss of her ponytail.

"Really?" Katani said coolly. She would love to have some of her things for sale at a classy shop like Dover Saddlery in Wellesley. It was one of the best riding apparel stores around. Katani moved to Penelope's back hoof to avoid Whitney's penetrating eyes. This so-together girl was making her nervous.

Whitney walked behind Penelope, pinning her hair back in place with the barrette. "See, I do know a thing or two about being an entrepreneur."

Katani could feel Whitney's eyes traveling up and down her. Prickles ran along Katani's back. Yikes! She realized that Whitney was as competitive as she was. Maybe she shouldn't have mentioned the contest to her.

"Like I said, I'd be happy to help you," Whitney continued. "I mean, if you're doing scarves, we could put our products together and market them as riding accessories." Katani had to admit that sounded like a great business idea, but she really wanted to do this all by herself. Especially without help from some snobby girl who already had her own successful business. Besides, if she won, she wanted the award to be all hers.

"Uhh . . . no thanks, Whitney," Katani finally spit out.

As she bent down to clean Penelope's last hoof, Katani sneaked a glance at Whitney. Did she actually look a little bit . . . hurt? Katani suddenly felt guilty for blowing her off, but immediately a bright, fake smile filled Whitney's face.

"That's okay," Whitney said quickly. "Can you just let me know where the ad was for the contest?"

Katani opened her mouth, but before she said anything, Kelley was standing beside Whitney, blurting, "*T-Biz!*, *T-Biz!* The 'Entrepreneur of the Year' contest encourages young entrepreneurs to develop their expertise to successfully start and manage their own businesses. This is an opportunity for all young entrepreneurs to fulfill their dreams," Kelley repeated the contest ad in a monotone voice.

Katani gripped on to Penelope's mane and slowly counted to ten. Kelley's incredible memory was about to make her scream.

"Mr. Bear and I, two business leaders of the next generation," Kelley went on.

Katani ignored Kelley and looked at Whitney, who seemed amused by all this.

"Thanks, Kelley. And good luck in the contest." Whitney smiled, showing her straight white teeth. "I'm sure you and Mr. Bear will do great."

Very funny, Katani thought. Whitney was so totally condescending.

"See you in two weeks." Whitney spun around and walked away from them, her ponytail swishing across her back.

"I like her, I like her very much. And Mr. Bear likes her, and Wilbur—"

"Kelley," Katani interrupted, and said as patiently as she could, "I should have told you the contest is a special pinkie-swear secret."

Kelley's eyes widened. She loved pinkie-swear secrets.

"You know what that means, right?" Katani asked.

Kelley nodded and sealed her lips with her finger. Then they hooked and unhooked their pinkies three times.

"No one else can know now," Katani warned her sister as she put her finger to her lips and pretended to throw away the key for emphasis.

Penelope stomped her hoof to the barn floor, reminding Katani to return her to her stall where food was waiting. As Katani led the horse back, Penelope nuzzled her shoulder. Katani whispered that she'd see her in one week and six days and stroked her neck. When Katani and Kelley stepped outside into the bright sun, the Triple B was heading toward the barn. Grandma Ruby waved to the girls as she splashed the big, blue Buick through the puddles.

Before she was inside the car, Kelley proudly announced, "Katani and I have a pinkie-swear secret! Don't even *ask* me what it is because I can't tell you. Big secret. No one else can know. NO ONE." Kelley made the whisper sign and shook her head.

Katani slunk down into her seat as Mrs. Fields gave her the eye.

CHAPTER

4

A Date or Not a Date

As she walked through the door of Montoya's and breathed in the rich smells of Cuban coffee, chocolate, cinnamon, sugar, and butter, Charlotte swore she dreamed about this place last night. She almost wanted to lick her lips in anticipation of a sip of the rich, dark hot chocolate that was Montoya's specialty. As Nick waved to her from behind the counter, she had to admit he was another reason why she liked coming here so much. Charlotte saw Avery, Maeve, and Isabel were waiting at the BSG's usual table in the corner, so she rushed over.

"Where's Katani?" she asked her friends. "She was supposed to meet us here before school, right?"

"Maybe Kelley didn't want to go to school alone today or something," Isabel suggested.

"But she would have called, no?" Maeve asked.

"I don't know about you guys, but I'm starving." Avery started over to the counter. "I've been thinking about their cranberry nut muffins since I woke up."

"I'm going to get the Isabel Regular: *buñuelos* and a

hot chocolate, topped with my personal fave—whipped cream with shaved chocolate on top, spiced delicately with a burst of cinnamon," Isabel said in a professional waitress voice.

"*Of course,*" the others chorused at the same time.

After they ordered and were carrying their breakfast treats back to their table, Nick called from behind the counter with a smile, "You're not going to start flying through Montoya's, are you, Maeve?"

"That was soooo funny." Avery started laughing all over again.

"I'm so glad I was at the rock gym to witness it, because I def wouldn't have believed it otherwise," Isabel added.

"Haven't you guys ever heard of 'Method acting'?" Maeve explained, shrugging the teasing off. "Now if I ever have to fly in a movie, I'll know how it feels!"

"Well, I talked my mom into letting me sign up for the rock-climbing team, so I want to start practicing this week," Avery announced, popping a big bite of muffin into her mouth. For someone so small, she ate more than anyone Charlotte knew.

"Wow, Avery. You're going to be super busy. The exhibition game is Thursday, remember?" Isabel reminded her.

"Do I REMEMBER? It's all I'm thinking about! I'm so psyched to play there! I mean, the TD Banknorth Garden, how cool is that? Swoosh!" She fake-shot a basket. "Imagine playing during the Celtics' half-time!"

"We have practice every day this week," Isabel said, with much less enthusiasm. She and Avery had both made the Abigail Adams basketball team, but Isabel was less sure of making the exhibition team. "Coach is choosing only five people for Thursday's game, and I bet I won't be one of them."

"Dude, don't even go there!" Avery shouted. "You have to think positive."

Charlotte turned to Avery. "But how are you going to do everything, Ave?"

"No big deal. I'll figure it out!" Avery smiled. "I hope you all get tickets. I want you to start a wave when I get a basket."

They started laughing. Then Maeve jumped up and swept her arms through the air. Isabel, Charlotte, and Avery copied her from their seats.

Anna and Joline walked into the café at that moment, looking way too cool for anything like a wave. They eyed each other, smirking. "OMG," Anna said, "what is this? A BSG wave . . . how adooooorable."

"Catch, Anna!" Avery leaped up to make a quick pass with her napkin toward QOM #1 just as Nick walked toward their table.

He reached out his hand to block her shot. "Hey, Paul Pierce, you sure you're ready for the Garden?" he teased.

"Just you wait," Avery replied, secretly psyched that Nick had compared her to one of the Celtics' best players. "Abigail Adams is going to rock!"

Smiling, Nick turned to Charlotte. "You up for the new Omni show at the Museum of Science, Char?" he asked casually.

Charlotte froze in her seat. Did Nick Montoya just ask her to go to a movie with him? Stammering and flushing, she spit out, "The one about the Serengeti? That'd be awesome." *That'd be awesome?* Did she sound too excited? Charlotte knew her face was turning bright red—again. And the fact that her friends were hanging on to every word of this conversion definitely didn't help.

"How about this weekend?"

"Um, that sounds good. . . ." *Sounds good.* Why couldn't she ever think of anything more interesting to say?! Something like . . . "Let me check my calendar." *Now he knows I had no plans,* she thought.

"Great, I'll e-mail you the details."

After Nick walked away, Maeve leaned across the table excitedly. "Omigosh, Charlotte, are you going on an actual real live date with Nick Montoya?"

"No, that wasn't," Charlotte stammered, "official." She picked up her hot chocolate mug as if she could hide behind it.

"*Official?* What do you think you're going to get, a written invitation?" Avery blurted.

Charlotte half spit and half dribbled hot chocolate down the front of her new long-sleeved Boston University T-shirt.

"I'll get some soda water." Isabel jumped up.

Charlotte didn't dare look around to see if Nick had seen her too. But she couldn't stop herself. He smiled at her from across the room and gave the thumbs-up. She groaned. "Major klutz strikes again."

"What number is this?" Isabel asked.

"I'm not exactly sure." Charlotte laughed. "But, I've been recording all my major klutz attacks."

"For real?" Avery asked.

Charlotte nodded. "I'm going to publish my collection one day and hand it out to every middle-school student."

"That's brilliant," Maeve said. "I'm sure it'll be a smashing success."

"The name Charlotte Ramsey does sound like a bestselling author, doesn't it?" Isabel said.

"So, Charlotte Ramsey, when did you actually start dating

Nick Montoya for real?" Maeve demanded, in her best entertainment-newscaster impersonation.

Charlotte was sure she'd turned every shade of red by now. When would she ever get thicker skin? "Well, it's not exactly a date," she said, desperately trying to sound casual. "I mean, Nick and I were talking about starting an online travel club with Chelsea Briggs. You know, a website where kids from all over the world can post their adventures and cool information about their part of the world. He probably just wants to talk about that."

"So," Maeve asked in a conspiratorial tone, "is Chelsea going to the movie too?"

Charlotte shook her head. "Um, I don't think so."

"Okay, then," Maeve said, as if that settled it. "It sounds like true love to me. Oh, Nick, I mean Romeo, wherefore art thou? I just love the sound of that," the redheaded romantic sighed.

Avery threw a cranberry at Maeve. "Earth to Maeve. Reality check."

Maeve pretended to look surprised. "What, you don't think it's true loooove?" She faked a swoon, with one hand dramatically resting across her forehead.

"No!" said Avery. "Charlotte can have a boy 'friend,' you know. I've got lots of them."

Charlotte smiled gratefully at Avery, though now that Maeve mentioned it, Charlotte was confused—was this a real date or not?

"Love is so complicated." Maeve sighed and picked up her pastry. The other BSGs couldn't help but laugh. Their dramatic friend did have a way of turning life into a soap opera!

Suddenly, Katani dashed into Montoya's, out of breath. "Hey, girls! Sorry to be so late."

"Terminally late. We're all leaving now," Henry Yurt warned as he approached their table, shrugging on his coat. The Yurtmeister was both the class president and designated class clown. He always managed to be goofy and sweet at the same time. "We're going to be in big-time trouble if we don't get moving. Especially this pair of zombies." Yurt gestured toward the Trentini twins, who looked like they'd just woken up.

"You should do something about the school hours, Prez. Like start school around ten," Billy Trentini muttered sleepily.

The BSG laughed and cleared their table. Before they left for school, Isabel opened her notebook to make a quick sketch of a bird flying madly in circles and carrying a letter in its beak to drop into the mailbox below. She wrote, "Better late than never."

Isabel M.

Better late than never.

The Fastest Knitter This Side of the Charles River

The BSG walked to school with Yurt and the Trentinis, all of them blowing white clouds from their mouths. Charlotte could see Yuri's fruit stand up ahead. The rest of the group kept walking as Charlotte and Katani stopped to say hi.

"Nobody wants Yuri's fruit today?" The burly Russian wore a brown fur hat with earflaps that tied under his chin that looked super warm and a little strange; Charlotte wondered if he had brought it with him from Russia. "What the matter here? All people needs vitamin C, eh. Have orange, girls, on Yuri."

"Thank you, Yuri."

"Now go fast to school. Americans always hurry hurry. No time for hanging out." Yuri rubbed his hands together. He sounded gruff, but he was like a marshmallow inside. Charlotte remembered how concerned he had been when her landlady, Miss Pierce, mysteriously disappeared. In fact, Charlotte suspected Yuri had a little crush on Miss Pierce! The girls each took an orange and hurried to catch up with the others.

"So, how are the contest plans going, Katani?" Charlotte asked.

"Ugh, that's why I was late. I've been working like a madwoman on my business plan."

"What else do you need to do?"

"Well, I have to fill out the application form and create a sales plan, promotion plan, and a detailed budget. Also, I need a recommendation from a teacher, but Grandma Ruby can do that—though I haven't asked her yet. I want it to be a surprise. I was thinking of asking Chelsea Briggs to take photographs of my final product." Reciting the list out loud, Katani felt suddenly anxious, but she pushed the feeling aside. She didn't have time to be nervous, and she didn't want anyone to think that she couldn't pull it off.

"At least I've decided what I'm going to make," she gushed on. "Scarves. Like the one I made for Grandma Ruby, you know?"

"That sounds like a lot of work, Katani." Charlotte wanted to sound realistic without putting a damper on Katani's enthusiasm. "We have an English project due soon—"

"I can't think about that right now," Katani said dismissively. "Besides, I'm a fast knitter, and I've worked out most of the designs. You've seen them, remember?"

Charlotte nodded. "They're great, and I know you're a champion knitter, but—"

Katani kept talking, hardly looking up. "There's just one snag."

Charlotte was beginning to think there might be more than one snag with all that work. It sounded too ambitious, even for Katani, but since she had refused any offers of help, Charlotte didn't dare say anything that might squelch Katani's plans.

"The only thing is," Katani continued, "I need to get some kind of hook, something that ties in with a community service. But I'll figure that out."

"And you've got to do all this by *when*?" Charlotte asked.

Katani hesitated, and her voice dropped when she told her the date that the application packet had to be postmarked. For the first time Katani didn't seem quite so assured.

"You really think that's possible?" Charlotte asked in a soft voice.

"It has to be."

CHAPTER

5

Competition Fever

Katani pushed through the usual morning chaos of the
AAJH hallways to get to her locker. Mondays were
always the worst, but with all that was going on, Katani
felt like today might possibly go down in history as one of her
worst Mondays ever. She straightened the photo of the BSG
on her locker door that Mrs. Madden had taken at Avery's
soccer game last fall. After the game, all the girls had posed
lying on the grass with their heads forming a circle, smiling
as they squinted into the sun. Katani sighed. She wished she
were lying on the grass with the BSG right now.

Oops, Yurt alert! President Yurt strutted down the hall,
high-fiving everyone he passed. He probably considered it
part of his job as class president, Katani thought with a hint
of frustration. Sometimes Henry Yurt was a bit much to take.
Especially when people had a lot to do! She turned back to
her locker so she wouldn't have to say hi to him.

"Extra-awesome shirt, dude." From the corner of her eye
Katani watched Dillon high-five the Yurt, who was wearing
his oversize Manny Ramirez jersey backward. Anything to

do with the Boston Red Sox was considered super cool at AAJH.

"Thought I'd do a test-run for 'Backwards Day,'" Yurt replied. "You know, to keep up AA school spirit."

A paper airplane went whizzing over Katani's head. Dillon jumped up and grabbed it. "Hey, Trentini," he yelled as he opened the piece of paper. "Isn't this your math homework?"

Down the hall, Betsy Fitzgerald, class know-it-all and one of Abigail Adams's best students, was distributing neon yellow flyers. Katani wondered what super-achiever Betsy was up to. Probably trying to persuade students they needed longer school hours or more homework or something. Katani had shut her locker and already started toward homeroom when Betsy intercepted her to hand her a flyer.

"Of course, you don't need my services, Katani, but you may know someone who does, so I'll give you a business card too."

In bold letters, the flyer read, **Super Test and Term Paper Prep with Bets: B or Better or Your Money Back**.

"You started your own tutoring business?"

Betsy nodded. "I'm submitting a business plan to this contest I saw in *T-Biz!* You know, that teen business magazine."

Katani hoped she didn't look as sick as she suddenly felt. She was sure her mouth was hanging open and her cheeks were burning. She felt like an idiot. Why had she assumed she would be the only one entering the contest? How many others from Abigail Adams alone would be submitting business plans? She suddenly felt like she was on a Tilt-A-Whirl.

"Here you go," Betsy said cheerfully. She handed a flyer to an eighth grader walking by. "Super Test and Term Paper

Prep with Bets: B or Better or Your Money Back. Contact: Betsy Fitzgerald, Honor Student."

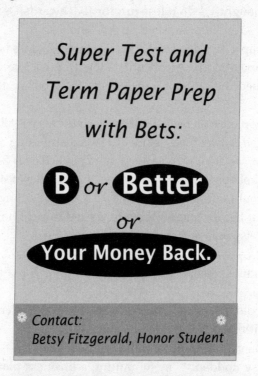

Super Test and
Term Paper Prep
with Bets:

B *or* **Better**

or

Your Money Back.

❀ *Contact:*
Betsy Fitzgerald, Honor Student

Katani held up Betsy's business card. In blue ink on smooth, creamy cardstock, it read, "Betsy Fitzgerald, Master Tutoring" with her contact information. Her presentation was so neat and smart, Katani guessed they had to have been professionally designed. In the center of the card was a logo of a stack of books. Of course anyone with a business should have business cards. Katani felt like crying.

"There's this community service part of the contest," Betsy blabbed on, "so I thought I'd charge on a sliding scale. So those who can't afford my services can still take advantage of them. I mean, even people who don't have much money should pay a little. That way it won't feel like I'm just doing them a favor, you know, and they won't feel like they can't ask a question. You know what I mean? "

"Yeah, sure," she mumbled. Betsy was so nice, you didn't want to hate her, but she could be so incredibly annoying. Katani saw Maeve standing next to Dillon, both of them reading Betsy's flyer. Mumbling a quick "see you" to Betsy, Katani ran to catch up to Avery and Charlotte as they headed toward homeroom.

"Did you guys see Betsy's flyer?" Katani whispered.

Charlotte nodded. "*So* Betsy."

"Tutoring schmutoring," Avery said. "Who has time?"

"Did you see how she packaged everything up so perfectly? She's applying for my contest too," Katani blurted.

Charlotte shrugged. "You know Betsy. It's all to get into Harvard."

"Knowing her, she probably already sent in her contest application," Avery snorted.

"Please don't say that." Katani's heart was racing now. She remembered her horoscope for this week, which she'd checked before she left this morning.

> *Virgo: Things are starting to happen for you. Once you get the ball rolling, do all you can to stand over your project and keep it in motion. Keep track of all important information, facts, and agendas.*
>
> *Don't get down on loved ones if they don't understand what you are trying to accomplish. Friends may be most helpful this week in lifting the burden of everyday chores. Little things will bring the greatest satisfaction.*

*Be careful of Mercury going into retrograde or
you may find you have a fried fuse.*

Just keep the Kgirl ball rolling, Katani told herself.

A Stellar Team

Later that morning, a distracted Katani sat in math class
two desks down from Betsy. She thought of all the things on
her list she had to do and felt like putting her head down on
the desk.

The night before, her mother had come into her room
to say good night, something she always did, no matter
how busy she was with her legal briefs. "Get some sleep,
sweetheart," she said softly. Mrs. Summers had leaned over
Katani's journals and papers spread across the bed to kiss her.
"You know what I tell myself on my busiest days? Something
Abraham Lincoln said: 'The best thing about the future is that
it only comes one day at a time.'" *One day at a time.*

Katani suddenly zoned back into math class. She realized
she hadn't been paying attention to Mr. Sherman, aka "the
Crow." He normally taught the pre-algebra math class, but
Katani's math teacher had invited him to speak to the algebra
class today, probably because he was the biggest math geek of
all the teachers. "Next week, your math projects will be due,"
the Crow intoned in his obnoxiously deep voice.

Uh-oh, Katani thought as her heart started pounding.
What math project?! How had she missed this?

Mr. Sherman went on, "As advanced math students,
everyone in this class is required to do a special research
project, which I supervise every year. The project should be
five pages and could include graphics, exercises, games—
however you want to present your material."

Katani glanced at Charlotte, the only other BSG in her math class, who also looked panicked.

"Be creative and have fun. Remember, math is the universal language," Mr. Sherman continued. "Next week, you'll present and teach your projects to the class. As you can see on the board, you have been assigned a partner to work with."

Katani saw her name beside Reggie DeWitt's, the math genius of Abigail Adams. *Wow*, she thought. *I totally lucked out.* But as exciting as working on this project with Reggie seemed, Katani didn't know how she could add it to everything she had to get done. Her head was spinning. Suddenly Mr. Sherman *did* look like a crow, just like Maeve insisted.

Maeve, who had to deal with the Crow every day during pre-algebra class, could do the most hilarious imitation of him, pacing back and forth with a menacing face. She'd flap her arms and say in a deep voice, "And now I'm going to swoop down on Maeve Taylor-Kaplan because she doesn't seem to understand that math is the most beautiful thing in the world. So I'll continue to say her name wrong and give math tests she'll flunk because she just doesn't G-E-T it." Then Maeve would start flapping her arms and fly around the room until they were all laughing hysterically.

When the Crow had the class break up to meet with their project partners, Katani saw Charlotte had been paired with Betsy! Of course Charlotte hadn't planned it, but Katani couldn't help resent the fact that they were already laughing about something. Charlotte was having too good a time with Katani's competition.

Reggie pulled a chair up to Katani's desk. She hadn't realized how green his eyes were, or that he had light freckles sprinkled over his nose. Reggie was cute up close, not like the intimidating genius he had always seemed like from far away.

"Hi, Katani. This is going to be totally cool. We're going to make a stellar team." His slender fingers tapped her desk. "Want to meet at lunch today to talk about the project?"

Maybe this would be okay. She'd just do the best she could. That was all she could do, Katani told herself.

"Sure, that sounds good," she told Reggie as the bell rang.

The Sound of Silence

Whenever Ms. Rodriguez waited for silence in the classroom like this, she meant serious business. Practically everyone in seventh grade at Abigail Adams loved Ms. R, but although she was young and friendly she also demanded that her students always do their absolute best on schoolwork. Everyone stopped talking, except for Joline, whose voice was suddenly loud as she exclaimed, "I'm totally sure he doesn't like *her*!" There was a smattering of laughter as Joline sat back, covering her mouth with her hand. The laughter was followed by a collective groan as Ms. R wrote "Book Reports" on the chalkboard.

Isabel frowned. She liked reading okay, but book reports were not her thing. She could never think of enough things to write about. When Isabel wrote, she struggled with each word. Her ideas came to her as images and pictures—not sentences. The world was so much simpler in pictures, she thought as she doodled on her notebook.

"The book reports should be on your favorite book and author. They should be five to six pages—"

There was another class groan.

Ms. R went on, "And they'll be due next Friday."

"Next Friday?" Dillon sounded incredulous. "Ms. R, you can't be serious. Are you trying to kill us?"

"Is it April Fool's Day or something?" Yurt asked.

"I'm not trying to kill you, and yes, I'm serious."

"Why don't you give us more time?" Anna whined. "Some of us have math projects due too!"

Isabel saw most of the kids in the class were slumped in their seats, including Maeve and Avery. Isabel sent Maeve, who looked like she was going to be sick, a sympathetic smile. Charlotte, queen of book reports, was already jotting notes. She looked like she couldn't wait to get started.

"Is everyone forgetting I told you a month ago that this project was coming up?" Ms. R said. "Having a tight deadline is a good lesson on planning your time carefully. Those of you who work on *The Sentinel* understand the nature of tight deadlines and how important they are."

"What about those of us who don't work on *The Sentinel* and don't understand the nature of tight deadlines?" Billy Trentini asked.

A few boys in the back guffawed.

"Let me finish. Learning to meet deadlines, short- or long-term, is a life skill we all need to practice," Ms. R said. "Now, are there questions?"

Riley, frontman for his own band called Mustard Monkey, raised his hand. "Can I do mine on *Mystery Train*, the greatest book on rock-'n'-roll ever written?"

"I'm glad you asked, Riley. Everyone must clear his or her book with me in the next few days. I'll give you time in class to brainstorm and plan your papers. By Thursday I'll expect you to have an outline and a short biography of your author. And see me after class about your idea, Riley."

Isabel zoned out as Ms. R went on about the specifics of

when everything was due. She really didn't have a favorite book. What could she write about?

Betsy's hand shot up.

"Yes, Betsy."

"I just wanted to let anyone who hasn't gotten one of my flyers know that I'm available for tutoring on a sliding scale. But I'm booking up fast and of course I need time to write my own paper."

Isabel could sense most of the class rolling their eyes. Katani, though, was staring with real intensity at Betsy.

"All right," Ms. R said, looking at Betsy with a bemused smile. "Now does anyone have a question specifically about the papers?"

The room was completely quiet.

6

Vacation Schmacation

Alone at the BSG lunch table, Charlotte was staring down at the clumps of macaroni and cheese on her tray when Isabel, Maeve, and Avery dropped their lunches on the table and plopped down beside her. "This doesn't taste as yummy as it usually does," Charlotte complained to her friends.

"I think it's the English paper. My lunch doesn't taste very good either." Isabel set her fork down on top of her tuna salad.

"Let's not talk about the English paper right now or I'll lose my appetite too," Maeve said. She held up her peanut butter and jelly sandwich on wheat bread. "My mom's on this I-can-do-everything-as-a-single-mom kick—make breakfast, lunch, and dinner for everyone, do all the shopping and cleaning, *and* work all day. It's, like, Mom, chill out already!"

"Want to trade?" Charlotte asked.

"Sure, if it includes your Jell-O."

Charlotte wiggled her cherry Jell-O side to side as she spoke to it. "It's so hard to let you go, delicious fake whipped cream and mouthwatering red goo blob, but I really love peanut butter. So . . . it's a deal."

Avery stopped chomping on her tomato-bacon-spinach wrap to say, "I can't believe Ms. R is giving us no time to write our papers. How could she do that to us, especially this week?"

"She did warn us a while ago that this paper was coming up," Charlotte reminded her.

"Char, no one listens to warnings except nerds. Present company excluded, of course," Avery said, making a funny face.

"The thing is," Isabel said, "even if Ms. R did warn us a month ago, she didn't give us any specifics so we could start the actual writing. It takes me *forever* to write anything. I wish I could do an art project instead."

"Well, actually, she did tell us to look on her Web page," Charlotte explained.

"Only you and Betsy remember that stuff, Char," Avery blurted. "Besides, I have no clue what I'm going to write about. I hate trying to figure out all the symbolism and meaning of things. Why can't authors just say what they mean already?"

"Didn't you just read a Martin Luther King biography that you said was great?" Charlotte asked her. "Why don't you write about civil rights issues and bravery and character?"

"Char, you are brilliant!" Avery stretched over the lunch table to give Charlotte a high five. "My stress level just went down about a hundred points." That was Avery, Charlotte sighed. You couldn't stay annoyed at her for long.

"I wish mine did," Maeve said glumly.

"Ditto," Isabel added.

"My mom knows all about Martin Luther King because her mother actually went on a march with him," Avery informed them as she crunched on a carrot stick.

"That's amazing," Charlotte said. "You'll have tons to write about. Maybe you can interview your grandmother?"

Avery nodded. She hadn't spoken to her Nana in a long time. This could be fun.

"Five to six pages is practically a novel," Maeve moaned. She pushed the macaroni and cheese around on her plate. "Besides, my favorite story of all time is *Romeo and Juliet*—the movie version, of course, with my big-time crush. Leonardo, in case you were wondering. Back in the day when he was young. Think the movie version will count?"

"It might," Charlotte answered. "Ask Ms. R. She wants us to choose something we really love."

"She probably doesn't want to read a bunch of boring reports," Avery pointed out in between bites of an apple.

"What are you writing yours on, Char?" Isabel asked.

"*Anne of Green Gables*," she said in a dreamy voice. "It's one of my favorite books in the whole world. My dad took me to Prince Edward Island to see the house and everything. I was eight and I wanted to stay and live there. I couldn't understand why we couldn't. When the tour was over, I ran into the Haunted Woods and refused to leave!"

Charlotte started laughing at the memory, and her friends did, too. They didn't notice Dillon and Yurt walking over to their table.

"Glad to see someone's still laughing after that English assignment," Dillon grumbled. "What's up with Ms. R, anyway?"

"Under pressure," Yurt sang the song by the band Queen. "Under pressure."

At that moment Betsy strode up to them, energetically passing out more flyers. "In case you didn't get one this morning."

"We'll all need extra help this week," Dillon said, taking another flyer.

"I get by with a little help from my friends," Yurt sang, switching over to the Beatles tune. "Gonna try with a little help from my friends."

"Dude, you're a walking karaoke machine!" Dillon said to Yurt as the boys headed back to their table.

Maeve read the flyer again. "B or Better." Hmmm. She really needed to get a good grade on this report, but . . . She brushed the disloyal thought from her mind.

"I really like your earrings, Isabel," Betsy said. "Are they new?"

"Actually they are." Isabel swung the bright blue orbs so they caught the light and were even more striking against her dark hair and eyes.

"They're beautiful," Betsy said.

"Thanks. My mom went out shopping and bought them for me."

Isabel's mother's multiple sclerosis often left her dizzy and tired. Mrs. Martinez rarely left her sister's house alone, so going shopping was a big deal for her.

"That's so great, Izzy. I read once that mild exercise is good for people with MS," Charlotte said. Charlotte, whose mother had died when she only four years old, was always concerned with Mrs. Martinez's health. Her concern made Isabel nervous sometimes, like maybe Charlotte thought something really bad was going to happen to her mom, too.

"I can't believe I didn't notice those before," Maeve said. "They're totally gorgeous."

"Probably because I just pulled my hair back, something I always do when I start to stress!" Isabel laughed a little.

"Well, let me know if I can help," Betsy told her. "See you this afternoon, Char."

They all turned to Charlotte as Betsy walked to another table to pass out her flyers.

"Isn't Betsy entering the same contest Katani is entering and therefore is her nemesis right now?" Avery spoke with increasing speed.

"Good word," Charlotte said with a laugh. "And I guess you could put it like that, though it's kind of harsh to define Betsy as Katani's enemy."

"Where *is* Katani anyway?" Maeve wondered. "It's way late."

"Maybe the library?" Isabel suggested.

"We have a five-page project due for math, too. She has two projects and the contest this week," Charlotte explained. Then she lowered her voice, looking guilty. "And Betsy's my math project partner."

"Uh-oh," Avery cautioned.

"Specially arranged by the Crow, I'm sure," Maeve said, rolling her eyes. "You know what I think? We all need to go on a fabulous vacation and forget about all this UN-fabulous work. What do you say, travel agent?"

Before Charlotte could answer, Avery called out, "Celebrity sighting—nerd station—Katani sitting with Math Boy!" She pointed across the crowded cafeteria.

"Katani and Math Boy?" Maeve repeated in surprise. "E News alert!"

Maeve's Notes to Self:
1. *Run by Irving's after school for Swedish Fish!*

2. *Watch* Romeo and Juliet *for the one-millionth time.*
3. *If humanly possible, start thinking about topic for the English paper.*
4. *Katani and Reggie???? Wuzzup!*

A Very Simple Plan

For the last five minutes Katani had been playing with her chicken and vegetable stir-fry left over from supper last night. She couldn't believe how easy it was to talk to Reggie. She felt more relaxed than she had all day. "We have an English paper due too. Five to six pages," she told him. "But I'm not that worried. I'm going to write on *Let the Circle Be Unbroken*, and I've read that about a hundred times. I love that book."

"Really? I just had to do one on *To Kill a Mockingbird*."

"That's a really good book," Katani enthused. "And the movie was incredible."

"I liked it too! I loved Boo Radley. If I had a band, I'd name it Boo Radley." Reggie finished his turkey sandwich and opened a bag of Marshmallow Treats, looking a little embarrassed. "My mom always packs something sweet. She thinks I'm going to forget to eat or something. Want one?"

"I'd never pass up one of these. Thanks." She popped the gooey treat into her mouth, and for no reason at all, blurted out, "I'm putting a business plan together."

"Really?" Reggie seemed genuinely interested.

"I've been thinking about business for a long time. I want to own a fashion design and advice company someday. But now I'm entering this young entrepreneur contest from *T-Biz!* magazine. I have to write out an entire business plan, the finances, marketing strategy, and show that I actually sold stuff." *Why am I telling him all of this?* she thought.

He'll probably want to join the contest too. Betsy, Whitney, Math Boy—the list was getting longer. She popped another Marshmallow Treat into her mouth. Maybe the treat would help her stop talking.

"Whoa. You're doing all that on top of school? That's, like, unbelievable."

Katani couldn't believe Reggie thought it was *unbelievable*. He was, like, the smartest person in the whole school, and he was impressed with *her*. She glanced over at the BSG table and started to feel panicky again when she saw Betsy chatting to her friends and passing out flyers. This was so unlike her. The Kgirl was always in control. Everyone always said how organized and together she was. But right now there were so many butterflies in her stomach, Katani actually wondered if people could see them fluttering.

"The closest I've ever come to running a business was a lemonade stand, and I drank most of my profits!" Reggie told her.

Katani laughed, trying to shake off her discomfort. She finished her Marshmallow Treat and said, "Maybe we should talk about our project. I really liked the Egyptian Math unit earlier in the year."

"I can't believe it!" Reggie's eyes gleamed. "That's totally what I was thinking! Just this weekend I found this really awesome website on Egyptian Math. That would be so cool! Let's meet at the library tomorrow right after school. Can you do that?"

"It's a plan." Katani smiled. It was so nice to have a partner who was already ahead of schedule.

CHAPTER

7

Stuck Like Glue

Temporarily banned from her bedroom so her older sister Elena Maria could have a major heart-to-heart with a friend from school, Isabel was sitting at the dining room table, attempting to do her homework. But instead of words on paper, there were bits of scrap paper covered with her doodles scattered around in front of her and on the floor.

Isabel's mother and Aunt Lourdes had volunteered to do the dishes so Elena Maria and her friend could have some extra time. Water was running and dishes were banging and Isabel could hear her aunt humming and occasional laughter floating out of the kitchen. The last few days had been good ones for her mother, and Isabel didn't want to ruin any of it on account of the major homework funk she was in.

Isabel looked at the clock. For the last twenty minutes she had been staring at a blank piece of paper and hadn't gotten anywhere. She didn't even know what book she was going to read. There were plenty of books she liked but none she wanted to write five to six pages on.

She looked up at the print of a painting by Frida Kahlo,

framed on her aunt's wall. She loved the bright colors of Frida's paintings. As she stared at the picture, all Isabel felt like doing was drawing and working on her art projects—and she wouldn't mind joining Avery on the rock-climbing team either.

One thing for sure was that she did not want to write a book report. She doodled a cartoon of a bird sitting on the edge of a nest, clearly not ready to make the leap, and wrote, "Did you ever just feel stuck?" Just as she put her head on top of her books on the table, her mother walked in.

"What's wrong, *chiquita*?"

Isabel never wanted her mother to worry about her. She and Elena Maria were supposed to make things easier for their mother. She was about to say, "Nothing, Mama," when she realized she really needed to talk to her mother.

"Well, the truth is, I can't do my book report for English. I have no clue what book to pick. I hate to write. . . ."

"Shhh," her mother said, taking a seat next to her and running her hand over Isabel's long, dark hair. "What'd your teacher say? What kind of book are you supposed to read?"

"We're supposed to pick a favorite book to write a five-to-six-page book report on. I can't do that. Book reports have too many words!"

"Why don't you choose one of those myths you love instead?" her mother wisely asked. "And then you could retell the story in a book with your own illustrations."

"Wow!" Isabel exclaimed. "That is an excellent idea. You're a genius, Mama!"

"Better get your teacher's approval first," Mrs. Martinez suggested.

"I'll ask tomorrow," Isabel promised. "I hope she says yes. I know exactly what myth I'll use: Icarus!"

Isabel first read the story of Icarus when she was visiting her grandparents in Mexico City a few years before. Her grandmother had read it in Spanish, and later Isabel read it in English. Isabel imagined herself with wings made of feathers and wax and thread like Icarus had. She could see why Icarus was tempted to fly too close to the sun—it was the most beautiful golden ball hanging in the Mexican sky.

Now pictures started forming inside her head of Icarus soaring too close to the sun, his wings melting, his feathers starting to fall into the sea. She picked up her pencil. She couldn't wait to get started!

The So-called Date

That night in her room, Charlotte knew she should have been thinking of ideas for the math project before she and Betsy met tomorrow after school. But she would much rather work on her book report. She kept remembering their visit to the Anne of Green Gables house on Prince Edward Island. She and her father had traveled so much since her mother died. As soon as she saw the farmhouse she'd read and dreamed about, it felt like the home Charlotte had wanted for so long. She'd envied Anne living on the farm with Marilla and Matthew, and she had secretly been in love with Gilbert for years.

Downstairs her father was preparing for a writing seminar he was teaching later in the week. He was also in the middle of a piece he had to finish by Friday for a travel magazine. As busy as he was, he did everything he could to make the Victorian house on Corey Hill their home because he knew how much it meant to Charlotte.

She glanced at the clock and thought she had better get going on her book report. She was starting to think that maybe she should reschedule the movie with Nick this weekend. There just wasn't enough time for everything. Sighing, Charlotte pulled out her well-worn copy of *Anne of Green Gables* and started taking notes on her favorite parts of the story. She was rereading the scene where Anne stops talking to Gilbert Blythe because he teases her about her red hair when she had a horrible thought. Would Nick stop talking to her if she said she couldn't go to the Omni show this weekend? Suddenly, she *had* to e-mail Sophie, her best friend in Paris.

TO: Sophie
FROM: Charlotte
SUBJECT: What should I do????

Ma meilleure amie,
I wish I could zap you here right now,
mon amie! We could walk to Montoya's for
a hot chocolate and I could tell you
everything.
Nick asked me to go to the Museum of
Science to see an incredible movie on
the Serengeti. Of course I'm dying to
see it, especially w/ him. We've had the
best talks about traveling to Africa and
everywhere else. The problem is I don't
know if it's a real date or not. Part
of me wants that & the other part of me
is shaking in my boots! He's such a nice
friend, and I wouldn't want to change
that. I don't know what to do or think!
Quel problème!
The other thing is, I'm really busy at
school this week, and our so-called date
(he never called it a "date" either!) is
in 6 days! Will Nick ask me to go again
if I say I can't go this weekend?? *Au
secours!*
Tell me about everything with you. It's
so cold here! I miss you! Give your
family *une accolade* from me.
Love,
Char

Who's Freaked Out?

Katani was sitting on her bed figuring out what it would cost to buy yarn and what she could charge for her scarves when her sister Patrice appeared in her doorway. "Telephone, Katani! And make it quick. I'm expecting a call." Patrice loved bossing her around whenever she got the chance. "Think fast!" Patrice laughed, tossing the phone to Katani.

Katani miraculously managed to keep from fumbling the phone.

"Nice catch." Patrice smiled.

Katani leaned back and put the phone to her ear. It was Marky, from High Hopes riding stable.

"I just wanted to check to see if you were going to sign up for Pony Camp this summer," she said.

"I totally forgot!" Katani had a sinking feeling in her stomach. She couldn't believe she'd completely forgotten to fill out the form, even after Claudia had reminded her.

"It's probably not too late," Marky reassured her.

"I've been so caught up in this contest. The deadline is so soon!"

"It is a really cool contest. I wish I had some business talent, but I don't." Marky sighed. "Did you know Whitney made three hundred dollars in one day at Myopia?"

"I know," Katani answered dryly.

"She told me she might enter the contest too."

I knew it! Katani fumed. That's all she'd wanted to do from the beginning: enter the contest herself. Her suspicions about Whitney were definitely confirmed. Katani felt her head go hot and she felt dizzy.

"Katani?" Marky asked. "Are you still there?"

"Sorry, I got distracted," Katani answered. "My sister has to use the phone."

"Oh. Well, I'll see you at the next lesson. Good luck with the contest!"

"Thanks, Marky."

As she hung up the phone, Katani felt like hiding in the closet with a blanket and Mr. Bear. First Betsy and now Whitney. Who else was applying to the contest . . . everyone she knew?

She looked over at the clock. The second hand seemed to be going faster and faster. Katani took a deep breath. She knew she had style and she thought she had the ambition and drive to make things happen. She was just going to have to work even harder on these scarves to make sure Kgirl was the number-one young entrepreneur.

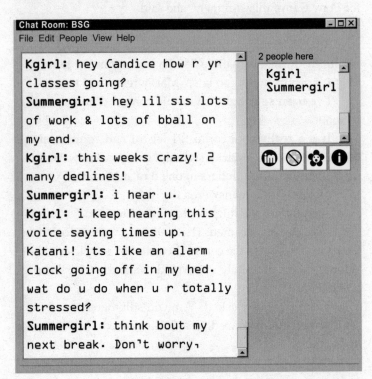

Chat Room: BSG

File Edit People View Help

Kgirl: hey Candice how r yr classes going?
Summergirl: hey lil sis lots of work & lots of bball on my end.
Kgirl: this weeks crazy! 2 many dedlines!
Summergirl: i hear u.
Kgirl: i keep hearing this voice saying times up, Katani! its like an alarm clock going off in my hed. wat do u do when u r totally stressed?
Summergirl: think bout my next break. Don't worry,

2 people here

Kgirl
Summergirl

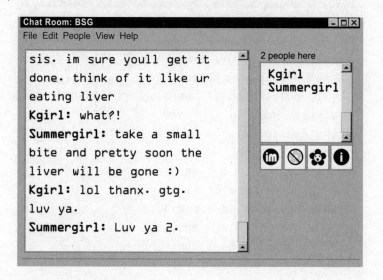

File Edit People View Help

sis. im sure youll get it done. think of it like ur eating liver
Kgirl: what?!
Summergirl: take a small bite and pretty soon the liver will be gone :)
Kgirl: lol thanx. gtg. luv ya.
Summergirl: Luv ya 2.

2 people here

Kgirl
Summergirl

"What are you doing, Katani?" Kelley asked, looking at the papers spread out all over Katani's bed.

"Working on our pinkie swear secret," Katani said.

"Me too!" Kelley said cheerfully. "I'm drawing outfits for Mr. Bear—you can knit them for us."

Katani stifled a groan. She wanted to shout, *No way, I have NO time, don't you get it?!* This was only the busiest week of her life! But just then her IM message bar flashed with a new message from the BSG. Katani couldn't wait to tell them all about Whitney and everything. But Kelley was still standing beside her, waiting patiently.

Katani took a manual on learning to knit and purl for beginners from her desk drawer and handed it to Kelley. "I'll teach you to knit—tomorrow, okay? You can look at this for now."

Smiling, Kelley held the book to her chest. "It's a date, a very important date!"

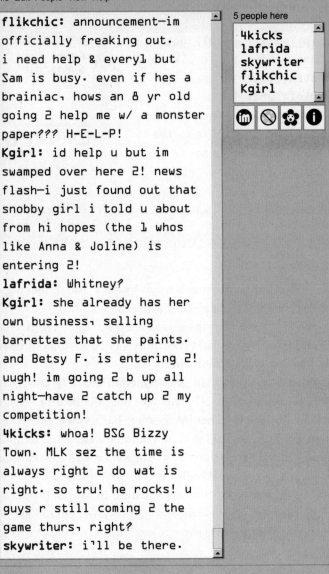

Chat Room: BSG

File Edit People View Help

5 people here

4kicks
lafrida
skywriter
flikchic
Kgirl

flikchic: announcement—im officially freaking out. i need help & every1 but Sam is busy. even if hes a brainiac, hows an 8 yr old going 2 help me w/ a monster paper??? H-E-L-P!

Kgirl: id help u but im swamped over here 2! news flash—i just found out that snobby girl i told u about from hi hopes (the 1 whos like Anna & Joline) is entering 2!

lafrida: Whitney?

Kgirl: she already has her own business, selling barrettes that she paints. and Betsy F. is entering 2! uugh! im going 2 b up all night—have 2 catch up 2 my competition!

4kicks: whoa! BSG Bizzy Town. MLK sez the time is always right 2 do wat is right. so tru! he rocks! u guys r still coming 2 the game thurs, right?

skywriter: i'll be there.

lafrida: i hope 2 b playing w/u!

flikchic: if I havent turned in2 a zombie or worse, ill b there 2 start the wave!

4kicks: thanx. im starting 2 get nervous

Kgirl: see u tomorrow—have 2 go!

flikchic: wait! oops—so much 4 getting any Kgirl tips 2 help w/ my paper

skywriter: have u done any brainstorming? just rite whatever comes 2 yr hed. dont edit or anything

flikchic: i dont even no if ms r will let me do it on the R & Juliet movie. i have 2 go 2. wish me luck!

5 people here

4kicks
lafrida
skywriter
flikchic
Kgirl

Maeve dumped her book bag out on her oh-so-pink bedspread and flopped back on her luscious pink heart pillows. *Thank goodness for all this delicious pink!* she thought, yawning. It was times like this when Maeve wished that all her learning problems would just float away in a giant pink balloon never to be seen again. Of course, one day she'd be famous and none of this school stuff would matter, she told herself as she let out a sigh the size of Texas. Unfortunately, she needed major 411 now.

She couldn't believe that her tutor, totally adorable Boston College student extraordinaire Matt Kierney, would choose this week of all weeks to be out of town. But if the BSG were too busy to help, who could she turn to?

She sat up and started flipping through the papers on her bed, trying to remember what other homework she had. She'd been so stressed out since English class, she hadn't even remembered to fill out her daily planner. Suddenly, she noticed a bright yellow piece of paper on the floor, half hidden under the bed. "Super Test and Term Paper Prep with Bets: B or Better or Your Money Back. Contact: Betsy Fitzgerald, Honor Student."

CHAPTER

8

A Little Pink
Fixes Everything

As soon as she arrived home from school the next day, Maeve pulled out a pint of strawberry swirl ice cream and a jar of Fluff and mixed them together until she had her favorite perfect pink concoction—Maevelicious Pink Pluff.

"That's so gross." Sam made a face. At the kitchen table, her eight-year-old brother was reading a book on the Civil War and eating a banana covered in peanut butter.

"*That* is disgusting," Maeve said, pointing at his mushy snack, which was smeared on the corners of his mouth.

"Maeve," her mother called from the dining room. "What are you two eating?"

"Just a little Pluff and banana gob. I need some energy to work on my English paper, and Sam is just being disgusting," she said in a syrupy sweet voice.

"Well, please keep it down in there. I have a lot of work to do this afternoon," her mom ordered.

"Okay, Mom." Maeve stuck her tongue out at Sam.

"Which was the first war to use submarines?" he asked with his mouth stuffed with banana.

"Yuck," Maeve said. "You shouldn't talk with your mouth full. That's gross."

"You don't know?" Sam asked. "Make a guess. If you guess, it I'll give you some gob!"

"Maeve and Sam," their mother called.

While Sam went back to reading, Maeve took her dish and book bag and headed for her bedroom. She couldn't stop thinking about what Dillon had told her on the walk home. Betsy had really helped him with his music paper on Beethoven. Now that Ms. Rodriguez had told her she could go ahead with her *Romeo and Juliet* idea, Maeve wanted Betsy to help her, too, but she was afraid that Katani would be totally offended. Dillon even said that Betsy was keeping files of all her "business" tutoring sessions to use as part of her submission package for the contest. Typical Betsy. It would be on record that Maeve had hired Katani's competition. *How could I do that to the Kgirl?*

Maeve glanced up at the photo of the BSG in the "Best Friends" frame on her night table. Dressed in black striped pajamas for Pajama Day at school, the girls had gone as jailbirds, ball and chained together. It had been so much fun! Maeve grabbed a pencil and began chewing on it. "Idea, come to me!" she intoned. Nothing! Maeve jumped up from her bed and ran to her guinea pigs' cage as visions of giant F's danced in her brain. She really didn't have any other option—she would have to call Betsy Fitzgerald, Tutor to the Desperate. First, though, she had to make sure it was fine with her mother, since she would be paying. "What can I do? Cleo and Caesar, I need help!" she wailed to her guinea pigs as she shoved aside a fleeting picture of a wounded Katani.

Pink Revelation

As Katani walked into Think Pink! she realized that Razzberry Pink's store displayed every shade of pink under the sky. The store always reminded Katani of something out of a fairytale. As she breathed in the sweet strawberry scent of the store, a lightbulb went off in her head.

Ms. Pink just had to say yes! But first, Katani had to wait until the store owner was finished helping a customer choose a pink suede handbag in the shape of a heart.

"My little niece is going to adore this," the woman gushed. "Ava loves pink more than anyone."

Except Maeve. Katani smiled as she sorted through the Think Pink! scarves. There were plenty of silk scarves in various pink patterns but only a single knitted one in plain wool. Her heart beat even faster. She could hardly wait for Ms. Pink to finish ringing up the lady's heart handbag, pink lizard earrings, a book called *We Are All Pink Inside*, and a jar of some kind of neon pink jam.

After the lady waved good-bye, Katani nervously approached the register. "Do you have a minute, Ms. Pink?"

"Of course." The young woman with the magenta pink hair smiled at Katani. She looked so chic in her marbled pink framed glasses, magenta pink polka dot T-shirt, tight glittery pink jeans, and pale pink leopard clogs. *Only Ms. Pink could carry that outfit off,* marveled Katani.

Katani decided to cut right to the chase. After all, she thought, businesswomen have to take risks. "I noticed that you didn't have a lot of winter scarves. I was wondering . . . umm . . . thinking, actually . . ." *Pull yourself together right now, Katani Summers,* an embarrassed Katani scolded herself. "I mean, I made a line of mohair scarves in various shades of pink. Like this one." She unwound the scarf around her neck and handed it to

Ms. Pink. *Now we're talking.* Katani felt in control again. "But with a beaded motif at the end. Do you think maybe you could you sell something like that?"

Ms. Pink fingered Katani's soft scarf. "Well, I think I could, Katani. We do need more winter scarves, and I love these . . . they're so . . . ." She smiled. ". . . deliciously pink. If you could bring in twenty of these by the weekend for Breast Cancer Awareness Week, I'll feature them at my fund-raiser for breast cancer research," she explained, and pointed to the poster behind the register.

Katani's mouth opened, but it took a few seconds for her to respond, "I think . . . I mean, I know I could do that."

"Think Pink! is a proud supporter of social causes. I want a portion of all our proceeds to go back into helping the community."

Katani nodded excitedly. This was perfect for the contest! Everything was falling into place.

"My grandmother Lulu died of breast cancer when I was just a girl," Ms. Pink went on, looking past Katani into the already darkening afternoon sky. "She loved pink too. You can't believe how happy it makes me that pink is the breast cancer research color."

Her gaze returned to Katani and she said, "I think your scarves will be a big hit."

There was one more important thing Katani had to ask. She summoned all her courage and blurted out, "Do you think you can give me a down payment on the order so I can buy the yarn?" Then she held her breath and crossed her fingers.

Ms. Pink glanced at the cash register. After what seemed like a long pause, she answered, "I will, but you'll have to get the scarves to me on time. Deal?"

"Deal."

"I'm having the fund-raiser on Sunday afternoon, so I'll need the scarves that day."

"All right." Katani could feel her fingers start trembling. As excited as she was, the reality was just beginning to set in. Twenty scarves by Sunday! She'd get them done no matter what, she told herself. As she looked at her watch, she realized that she better get to the yarn store right away.

Space Cake

Katani practically danced around JB's Bead, Yarn, and Craft store, filling her shopping basket with all the different shades of pink mohair yarn she needed. The way Ms. Pink had treated her like a real businesswoman gave Katani confidence and completely re-energized her about the contest.

As she picked up a skein of pale pink yarn, Katani heard the door open. She looked up to see, of all people, Whitney! What was she doing here? Katani ducked her head, pretending to stare intently at some sparkly beads. Whitney was absolutely the last person Katani wanted to see right now. When Whitney had disappeared into another part of the store, Katani hurried to the register to pay for her yarn and make an escape. But when she turned around, a shopping bag in each hand, Whitney was walking directly to her!

"Hi, Katani," she said matter-of-factly. "Mom, this is Katani, the girl from riding I was telling you about. The one who's entering the contest."

Tall and blond, Whitney's mom looked just like her daughter—cool, collected, and rich. Whitney's mom smiled to reveal perfectly white teeth. "Oh, yes, nice to meet you, Katani. You're just like Whitney—doing everything!"

Just like Whitney? Katani winced, then managed to put

on a small smile. "Nice to meet you. I thought you were Whitney's sister at first." People sometimes said this to Katani's mother, so she figured it would be the polite thing to say.

"Well, thank you very much! Whitney, I love your new friend!" She laughed. "Now, we need to get those beads you ordered. Do they have them behind the register?"

"They should. Thanks, Mom."

As soon as Whitney's mother was out of earshot, Katani blurted, "You're not entering the contest, are you?"

"You don't think I should?"

"It's not really fair."

As soon as Katani said this, Whitney looked wounded. Katani immediately felt guilty. She hadn't meant to sound so harsh.

"What do you mean, 'not fair'?" Whitney asked.

But before Katani could answer, Whitney's mother called, "Honey, could you take a look at these?"

"Okay, Mom, I'm coming." Whitney spun around and started walking away.

"Wait, Whitney—" Katani started.

"I'll see you at High Hopes," Whitney called icily over her shoulder.

Great, Katani thought. She hadn't meant to hurt Whitney's feelings . . . it just came rushing out. She stepped into the cold air outside the store, convincing herself that she had to say what she did to Whitney. Business was business, right? As Katani swung her two large bags of yarn toward home, she tried to shake off the feeling of Whitney's hurt eyes still on her.

Katani reminded herself that she should be happy. After all, everything was miraculously coming together. She had most of her business proposal drafted. Now she just had to figure out how she could knit those twenty scarves by the weekend. She was a super-fast knitter. She'd just have to work faster than she ever had before. She'd stay up all night if she had to. Candice said she sometimes pulled all-nighters at college. It couldn't be that bad.

Then, all of a sudden, Katani's hands went clammy. *Uh-oh.* Math Boy! She was supposed to meet Reggie after school to talk about their Egyptian math project!

Breaking into a run, Katani sprinted until she couldn't breathe. When she reached the entrance to school, she slowed to a walk so she could catch her breath. *Who knew yarn could be so heavy?* she thought as she flew down the hall to the school library, only to find the door closed. About to collapse, she leaned over, dropping her two big bags of pink yarn on the floor beside her, and tried to catch her breath. Her legs and feet were aching. Katani tried to swallow the lump in her throat. What should she do now? She'd made a terrible mistake.

She stood up at the sound of footsteps coming down the hall.

Arms crossed over his chest, Math Boy glared at her. "I can't believe you blew me off."

"Reggie, I'm really sorry, I—" Katani started.

"I was pretty psyched about this project, but it doesn't seem to matter that much to you." Math Boy's voice rose. "You know, I used to think you were serious about math and school and stuff. I mean, like you were up for a challenge, like me."

Katani opened her mouth to apologize again, but Reggie put his hands in his pockets and scowled at her. "You really let me down. I know our project could have been the best in the class. Not anymore."

Reggie turned his back to Katani and began walking

down the hall. Close to tears, Katani watched as Reggie's foot-steps got softer and softer and silence filled the hallway. Just a few minutes ago she was on top of the world. Now, Math Boy thought she was a complete loser.

Knit One, Purl One

Isabel was waiting with Avery in the school lobby after basketball practice when she saw Katani. Katani was looking down as she walked and didn't even notice her friends until she almost crashed into them.

"You okay, Katani?" Isabel asked.

Katani looked up, startled.

"Earth to Katani!" Avery laughed. "What are you still doing here?"

Katani put on a brave face for her friends. She hated it when people knew she was upset. "I was checking to see if I could catch a ride home with my grandmother."

"There's my mom. We'll give you a ride," Avery said. "Come on!"

"You sure you're okay?" Isabel asked as they walked into the cold afternoon air.

Katani nodded. "I just stayed up way too late last night."

"Ugh, me too." Avery opened the front door of her mother's SUV. "Hi, Mom. Can we give Katani a ride home, too?"

"Of course." Mrs. Madden turned to say hello to Katani and Isabel.

Avery was bouncing on the front seat. "I can't stop think-ing about the exhibition game. It's in two days! Coach Porter announces the final team tomorrow. I'm so rocked. There's just too much going on this week!"

"I told Avery it's not going to help to worry," Mrs.

Madden said as they drove away from the school. "If you girls are working too hard, you should have a time-out. We should stop at J. P. Licks or something like that."

"Sounds great!" Katani started, then thought better of it. An ice-cream break did sound perfect, but she really needed to get to work on those scarves. "But I should get home," she finished, in a disappointed voice.

"Same. I should help with supper," Isabel added glumly.

"All right, but remember," Mrs. Madden told the girls, "keep things in perspective and don't take too much on, or even small things can seem overwhelming."

Avery and Isabel started telling Mrs. Madden about basketball practice. It wasn't until they were driving down her street that Isabel noticed Katani hadn't said a single word since they'd left the school. Isabel was about to ask Katani how all her work was going when Katani's face became suddenly animated.

"I almost forgot, Izzy!" she exclaimed. "I need to get back those knitting needles you borrowed, if that's all right. I'll just need them for a few days, then you can have them again. I may have a few scarves going at the same time, you know, for the contest."

"Sure, no problem. Come in with me. You can say hi to my mother while I get them," Isabel said as they pulled up in front of Aunt Lourdes's house.

"Is that okay, Mrs. Madden?" Katani asked. "I'll be really quick."

"Of course, dear. Take your time." Katani smiled at Avery's mom. Mrs. Madden was so nice, even smiling when Avery turned the radio up really loud.

As soon as she opened the door, Isabel could smell the chili cooking. Her mother was sitting on the sofa knitting, like she had been for the last few days. Usually she would have been resting in her bedroom at this time. It made Isabel so happy to have her mother greet her when she walked through the door, she broke into a smile and ran to give her a hug. "How do you feel, Mama?"

She greeted Katani then turned to Isabel. "*Bien. Muy bien.*"

Isabel grinned with happiness. "What have you been doing?"

"Oh, just watching some talk shows while I work on this blanket," her mother said, shaking her head. "It's unbelievable, all these crazy people on TV! But I need background noise while I'm knitting."

"Just a minute, Mama. Mrs. Madden is waiting outside. I have to go get the knitting needles I borrowed from Katani. Be right back." Isabel dashed out of the room.

Katani was impressed by the neat, steady *click-clacking* of Mrs. Martinez's needles. *She knits even faster than me,* Katani thought, a little envious. "What are you making, Mrs. Martinez?" she asked, coming over to the couch to get a better look.

"Oh, it is just a baby blanket. Isabel has a new little cousin," she replied with a weary smile. "Which reminds me. Thank you so much, Katani, for loaning Isabel those knitting needles. Mine are nearly always in use, as you see."

"No problem," Katani reassured her.

"Are you starting some new project that you need them back now?"

"Well . . ." Katani considered whether she should tell Mrs. Martinez about the contest and the impossible pile of knitting she had waiting for her at home. As she looked into Mrs. Martinez's kind brown eyes, she knew she could trust her.

"The thing is, I kind of do have a problem," she said

in a low voice. "I promised to knit twenty scarves by this weekend for this contest I'm entering, and I haven't even started yet."

"Oh, that is a problem," Mrs. Martinez agreed, looking concerned. "Twenty scarves? That is a lot for a girl who also has to keep up with her schoolwork, family, and friends." She gave Katani a knowing look.

"I know," Katani said, looking down.

"But," Mrs. Martinez continued, leaning in and speaking in a low voice as well, "I think I might be able to help you."

"Really?"

"Well, I don't feel very well sometimes, but I do have two good hands here." She smiled, and it dawned on Katani what she was proposing.

"You would do that? You would help me knit?" Katani asked incredulously.

"Of course!" Mrs. Martinez's smile was getting bigger. "To tell you the truth, Katani, I get tired of watching TV and letting everyone else do things for me all the time. It would make me very happy to be able to do something to help someone else."

"It would be a huge help to me," Katani agreed. All of a sudden she felt hopeful.

"I'm sure I could knit at least three by this weekend," Mrs. Martinez offered.

"Thank you!" Katani exclaimed. Then her face darkened again. "Oh, but, Mrs. Martinez, if you could maybe not mention anything to Isabel . . . I'm trying to do this on my own. You know—a surprise for everyone."

"Your secret is safe with me, Katani," Mrs. Martinez reassured her. "You will bring me the yarn that you would like me to use and a sample scarf?"

"Yes, absolutely. I'll get it to you as soon as I can. I have the yarn in the car . . . but if I bring it in now, Avery and Isabel will see. . . ."

"Don't worry, Katani. Just give it to me when you bring the sample."

"Thank you so much!" Katani was glowing. Three scarves down, only seventeen to go!

Isabel rushed back in, holding the needles out. Katani and her mother suddenly got quiet, and she felt like she was interrupting something. *That's weird,* she thought briefly as she handed over the knitting needles.

Katani looked at her watch. "I better go," she said, and started toward the door with the knitting needles. "Nice to see you, Mrs. Martinez. See you tomorrow, Izzy."

TO: Charlotte
FROM: Katani
SUBJECT: Wat do you think?

Hey Char,
Need 2 ask u sumthing. remember whitney
from high hopes? The 1 who reminded me
of Anna and Joline? well, I saw her
at the yarn store 2day. I told her it
wouldn't be fair if she entered the
contest—should I have sed that?
w/b soon! thanx—
Kgirl

9

Who's the Genius Now?

Maeve paced around her room, picking up a glass figurine, a stuffed bunny, and a picture of the BSG. She eyed her "crush alert" wall, starring a poster of Orlando. Betsy would be over in five minutes. It would be so strange to have *the* Betsy Fitzgerald right here in her bedroom! *I better straighten up,* she thought as she began anxiously shoveling things into her drawers. She didn't want Betsy thinking she was a total disaster.

Maeve was still worried that she was betraying Katani by having Betsy tutor her. But Katani could finish her work without help from anyone. That's the way she was. "But that is not the way I am," Maeve said out loud. Still, she knew Katani well enough to know that she would be, if not angry, at least hurt. How could she understand Maeve really needed help when she never did?

The idea of an angry Katani made Maeve even more nervous. She should have talked this through with the BSG. Now it was too late. Betsy would be here any second.

Just then the doorbell rang. Maeve rushed downstairs

and opened the door to find Betsy standing there with a worn leather briefcase.

"Hi, Betsy," Maeve said. "You look so . . . so professional."

"Thanks." Betsy shrugged. "It's my mom's. My files don't fit in my backpack. I have to keep all this tutoring stuff straight."

"I thought maybe you were going to try to sell me something!"

"Oh, no!" Betsy looked shocked. "Just tutoring!"

They laughed, breaking the awkwardness between them. Then Maeve said, "Let's go to my room before my little brother comes out to spy on us."

Upstairs, Betsy's eyes widened and she stood frozen in the doorway of Maeve's pink palace. "I love this!" she exclaimed. "It's so, um, wonderfully pink in here! You could open your own Think Pink!"

"No, being onstage is my dream."

"I feel like I should put on my sunglasses. It's so dazzling!" Betsy pointed to the pink shelves of ribbons and trophies. "Did you win all those?"

Maeve nodded. "I've been taking dance practically my whole life."

"You must be really good at it."

"Better than math!" Maeve agreed, giggling.

"We better get started," a suddenly nervous Betsy said. They'd agreed to spend the first half of the session on math and the second on the English paper.

As Betsy spread all her material out on Maeve's desk, Maeve noticed her tutor glance up at her "cute boy alert" wall.

"Who's your favorite?" Maeve asked.

"Definitely Orlando."

"Really?" Maeve never would have guessed that about studious Betsy!

"I adore him," Betsy admitted, blushing a little. "But back to tutoring." Betsy was nothing if not focused. "We can start with your homework and go from there."

Maeve smiled and opened her book. Step by step, Betsy went through the first problem so Maeve could actually follow it. Then she said, "Okay, why don't you start the next one. Don't worry if you forget something. I'm going to walk you through it."

Maeve looked down at the swirl of numbers and then back up at Betsy. "I could show you a couple of dance moves if you want."

"Really?" Betsy looked surprised. Then her eyes fell on her watch. "Maybe when we're done. But I'm not much of a dancer. Let's keep going. What would you do next here?"

When they got to problem number three, Maeve couldn't stop herself from asking, "Did you like Orlando better in *The Lord of the Rings* or *Pirates of the Caribbean*?"

"Oh *Pirates*, definitely."

"Me too!"

The girls stared at the poster of Orlando with his moussed hair, black hoodie, and adorable grin.

"He's so cool, and those eyes," Maeve gushed. "He always seems like he's staring right at me!"

"Maybe we should start on the English paper?" Betsy suggested.

Maeve sighed. "We could."

"Okay." Betsy pointed to Maeve's shelves beyond the poster. "Is that a Magic 8 Ball, by any chance?"

"Yes." Maeve was afraid Betsy would think it was sort of silly.

"I had one too. I used to be obsessed!"

"I totally was!" Maeve practically shouted. She couldn't believe she had this in common with Betsy too. Orlando and the Magic 8 Ball. Who would have guessed?

"Don't tell anyone this, but I used to ask mine if I'd be the first woman president," Betsy said. "I'd ask about once a day until I got the answer 'Signs point to yes' or 'Without a doubt.'"

"I asked if I'd win an Oscar for Best Actress!" Maeve exclaimed. "That's my number-one dream." She smiled. "Should we ask it a question now?"

Betsy looked at her watch again. "Maeve, we have to get back to work. Time is flying, and we've barely gotten anything done!" Betsy straightened the piles of papers in front of them. "I haven't been very professional. I haven't even taught you anything yet!"

Maeve looked guiltily at her math homework. "Number three."

Betsy frowned and tapped her pencil nervously. "Do you think we could move to the kitchen to study? I can't seem to concentrate with all this, um, pink in here."

"That's funny. Pink totally relaxes me. In fact, I think I'd do much better in school if all the school walls were painted pink," Maeve said. "But sure, we can move if you think it'd work out better."

In the kitchen, the girls spread their papers and books out on the wooden table and got down to business. It was a great place to work. They went through Maeve's math homework until it really started to make sense. By the end, she was actually doing each problem on her own with Betsy's encouragement. Betsy was almost as good a tutor as Matt.

Maeve smiled when they finished. "You know, I actually hope the Crow calls on me tomorrow."

"Mr. Sherman?" Betsy asked.

Maeve wrinkled her brows and flapped her arms until Betsy was laughing. "Okay, you're right! He does look like a crow."

Next, they made a list of everything Maeve needed to do to organize her *Romeo and Juliet* project, including a visit to the library after school the next day. Betsy had seen the movie version, too. "It's really amazing that this play has been remade so many times," Betsy said. "It never gets old."

"It's so totally romantic. Love doesn't change!" Maeve swept her hand across her heart.

"Yes," Betsy agreed. "Language changes, clothes change, hairdos change, but human nature doesn't. That's why Shakespeare's plays are done over and over again."

"I could perform the Maeve version!" Maeve decided right then. "Do you think Ms. R would go for it?"

"She's pretty open. I bet she would. It might help to type out your idea now so you can present it to her on paper. Also, then you can just keep going when you go to write your version of the play. Just getting a couple sentences down always helps me."

"Good idea." Maeve opened her laptop and started typing her ideas for *Romeo and Juliet*, starring who else but Maeve and Orlando. It was her fantasy, right?

Sam walked into the kitchen. He opened the refrigerator and stared into the snack drawer.

"Sam," Maeve reprimanded, "you're interrupting us!"

Sam ignored her and pulled out the peanut butter from the cabinet. "That's why people spend so much time reading history, you know," he said.

"Why exactly is that?" Maeve asked, annoyed.

"History repeats itself. Like what you were talking about

before. What changes and what doesn't. But I didn't mean the love stuff."

"You were spying on us!" Maeve yelled.

"I was just doing my homework in the dining room like Mom said to." Sam turned to Betsy. "It's like the way armies attacked Russia in winter and they always got defeated, but they kept trying it, anyway."

"That's so true," Betsy said. "Wait, how old are you?"

"Eight."

"He's read about every battle under the sun," a proud Maeve told Betsy. "But I'm sure he doesn't know anything about *Romeo and Juliet*," she added just to make sure her brother's head didn't get any more swelled.

"I know in the movie you watched they use guns instead of swords and there are skyscrapers instead of castles, but it's the same story that Shakespeare wrote in 1597. It's the archetypal love story."

"How do you know *that*?" Maeve demanded of her brother, who sounded like he was suddenly forty years old.

"I read it after you rented the movie for the hundredth time."

"I'm so impressed!" Betsy's eyes brightened. "When I was your age I memorized every capital of every state and country in the world. Ask me one."

Brainiac meets brainiac, Maeve thought as Betsy and Sam quizzed each other. They were in heaven talking about how much they knew. Maeve hit the return button a few times and typed a note to herself:

Maeve's Note to Self:
   1. arkitipal (sp???) love story—ask Char what that
      means tomorrow!

2. *Okay, just because I'm not in the smart club, doesn't mean I don't know anything!*
3. *As annoying as he can be, Sam is a genius, which means I'm related to a genius, which I guess is cool enough for me!*

A Very Important Date

Katani knitted in front of her computer, waiting for Charlotte to reply. Where was that girl? Actually, Katani really loved to knit. While she worked she tried to decide what she was going to write about for her English paper. She knew *Let the Circle Be Unbroken* inside and out, but she couldn't focus on the story. Every time a thought came to her, she started thinking about Whitney and Betsy, the deadlines for her math project (she didn't even want to think about Reggie), the English paper, the contest, and dropping off twenty scarves to Ms. Pink. She tried to figure out how many hours she would need each day to complete all her projects. Maybe there really weren't enough hours. She wondered if there was a way you could expand time.

Catching a dropped stitch, Katani was grateful that Mrs. Martinez was going to knit three of the scarves. Katani would have to do two scarves a night and then knit all night on Friday, all day on Saturday, and all morning Sunday if she was going to make the deadline. Katani called Isabel's mom after dinner to let her know that she would drop off the yarn tomorrow. Fortunately, Isabel hadn't answered the phone, and Katani knew that her secret was still safe with Mrs. Martinez.

Suddenly her computer made the familiar *ping*. There was an e-mail in her in-box. Finally.

```
TO: Katani
FROM: Charlotte
SUBJECT: RE: Wat do u think?

K,
I remember u talking about Whitney
It's hard 2 say. Would u want to enter
the contest if u heard about it from
Whitney?
X 0
Char
P.S. Where have you been?
```

Katani hadn't thought of it like that. What if it were the other way around? Would she have wanted to enter the contest no matter what? But it wasn't the other way around. Katani had found out about the contest on her own. Besides, Whitney already had her own business and fancy riding clothes. Katani felt a little guilty for thinking that way, but still . . .

Kelley ran into their room right then. "I finished the book!"

"What book?" Katani asked without looking up.

"*Learning to Knit and Purl for Beginners*! I'm ready for my lesson." Kelley stood too close to Katani. "I'm not late for a very important date!"

Katani wanted to say no, but she knew this would only get Kelley upset and make everything worse. She counted slowly to ten, concentrating hard on her knitting. Then she sighed. She had to show Kelley how to knit. That was what her dad called doing the right thing.

"Okay," Katani said. "I said I'd show you, so I'll show you. Come on, we'll try it on the yarn I'm using."

"Why do you have so much of it?" Kelley asked, looking at the bag of pink mohair.

"I have to knit a lot of scarves, that's why," Katani said. Twenty seemed impossible. "Now let's start."

Kelley's stitches were loose and sloppy, but she caught on so quickly, Katani was astounded. "You really did read that book, didn't you?"

"Yes, I did," a very serious Kelley answered. "Do you need help with your scarves? Because I could help you."

Katani's mouth opened. Kelley was going to help *her*?

Chocolate Break

Charlotte needed a break from her paper. She took a chocolate Kiss from her desk drawer and checked her e-mail. Finally there was something from Sophie!

```
TO: Charlotte
FROM: Sophie
SUBJECT: Re: What should I do????
```

Mon amie,
Sorry to take so long time to write.
Like you say in America, I am busy!
Grand-mère was visiting here in Paris.
She is back at her house as I write to
you. She is very well, but I miss her.
She tells the best stories and makes
tarte aux pommes—my favorite.
In regard to your message, it sounds
like a date to me! I know you—you
better reschedule the date as soon as

```
your math project and book report are
finis.
More very soon, I promise.
Bisous,
S.
```

A date! Sophie thought Nick had asked her on a date. Charlotte wondered what she was supposed to do now.

The Aftermath

The next morning Katani was late for class. First she had to drop off the yarn and model scarf for Mrs. Martinez. Then she had to leave a note in Reggie's locker to apologize for being late to their library date. *Making myself late because I'm apologizing for being late—can it get much worse?* she thought hopelessly as she pushed the note through the vents on Reggie's locker before dashing away to homeroom.

Later that day, Katani got to math class early to give Reggie an opportunity to talk to her. But Reggie avoided looking in Katani's direction for the whole class. Mr. Sherman was there to check on their progress, and everyone else in class was talking about what they were doing. She cringed when she saw Betsy and Charlotte exchange notes.

She hoped that the printouts on Egyptian math she had gathered would show Reggie that she meant business, but right after the bell rang, Mr. Sherman asked Katani if he could talk with her in his classroom next door. After the last student left the classroom, Mr. Sherman stood behind his desk, rubbing his thick, dark brow.

"I thought you and Reggie would make a good team for this math project," he said, "but Reggie came to me this morning saying he didn't want to work with you."

"What?" Katani's cheeks went hot. How totally humiliating—she was getting dumped by Math Boy! This was beyond a bad day.

"Yes. So I've decided—because of the time—to let you submit separate projects. Reggie is going to work on Egyptian math." Mr. Sherman paused. "He said that was his idea. And he mentioned you were entering a business contest for young entrepreneurs. I assume you have a financial strategy and that sort of thing."

"Yes, I do," Katani mumbled. She was still trying to deal with the idea that Reggie didn't want to be her partner. What made him think he could just drop her like that? Just because she forgot one appointment? Katani could feel her temper rising.

"I'll let you submit your business plan for your math project then. It'll have to be five pages like everyone else's and you'll have to present it to the class. It'll show how math factors into real life." Mr. Sherman stopped frowning to add, "I'm impressed, Katani. Most kids aren't thinking of running their own businesses in seventh grade."

"Thank you, Mr. Sherman."

"You better go to lunch now."

Katani was grateful to be able to submit her business plan as her math project, but before she left Mr. Sherman's classroom, she felt her face burning again. She had never let a partner down on an assignment before, but she only missed an appointment. She just had a lot on her plate. If only Reggie would have let her explain. By the time she reached her locker, she was furious with Reggie.

Instead of going to lunch, Katani headed to the library, where at least she could tackle a piece of her business proposal and avoid any inquiring minds in the cafeteria. What if Reggie told everyone? She could just hear Anna and Joline whispering. The QOM loved this kind of stuff. She reached a hand up to her cheek. Maybe she was coming down with a fever.

Katani nodded to the librarian as she made her way to the back table. Before she sat down, she took out her three colored folders and her clipboard with the contest application from her bag and organized them in front of her, setting the financial papers on top. But she couldn't concentrate on anything. At Ms. Pink's store, Katani had felt like she was on top of the world, but now she was beginning to feel like she was in the bargain basement of life.

10

Time Out for Hot Chocolate

The sound of dribbling and sneakers screeching echoed through the gym. Coach Porter blew her whistle. "One more round of layups, then we'll go into scrimmage mode, everybody!"

"I can't believe the exhibition game's tomorrow," Anna whispered to Amanda Cruz.

"You know it's going to be on the news? I, like, sooooo want to be on TV!" Amanda squealed.

"Like who doesn't?" Anna responded in her trademark "I am so superior" tone of voice. But then, faking an uninterested tone, she asked, "Do you know how many people will be watching?"

"What do you care, Anna, if it's not such a big deal?" Amanda asked with a smirk.

Avery couldn't believe the two of them. Tomorrow was the day of the big game—they needed to focus and stop with the put-downs. Twenty-eight more hours until she and her teammates would be on the court at "the Garden." She glanced at Isabel, who was ahead of her in the layup line behind Anna and Amanda. The line was moving fast as her teammates dribbled toward the basket, one by one. When it was Isabel's turn, she drove to the basket. Her layup hit the rim and bounced twice before falling back to the floor. Avery clapped hard, anyway, and shouted, "Let's go, Abigail! Let's do it!"

The team was really pumped for the next day's game, and energy was high in the gym. Avery's hands were sure as she caught the ball, dribbled in and *swish*! She nailed it! After practice, Coach Porter was going to announce the five players who would be playing in the exhibition game. All the girls were nervous, because they really wanted to be picked. During the scrimmage, some players were trying to show off, hoping Coach would choose them at the last minute.

After ten minutes of scrimmaging, Coach Porter finally blew her whistle. "Okay, Abigail Adams, break!"

When they were all gathered around, their coach said, "As you know, we're stopping a little early today to talk about tomorrow's game. Choosing five of you to play has been a very difficult decision. I hope all of you who haven't been chosen will come and support the five who have. The most important thing to remember is we are a team, one team. Abigail Adams."

Coach Porter folded her arms across her chest and said, "If I call your name, please stay here for a few minutes. Everyone else can head to the locker room." She paused as she consulted her clipboard. *Hurry up!* Avery thought impatiently. The coach finally went on, "Okay. The five who will play tomorrow night are Amanda, Avery, Julie, Sarah, and Anna."

Avery looked straight at Isabel, who shut her eyes and squeezed her hands into fists. *Uh-oh*, Avery thought.

She wanted to run over right then and do something—
ANYTHING—to make Isabel feel better. Like tell one of her
famously corny Avery Madden sports jokes! Isabel loved
those. But Coach had asked them to stay. Avery watched
helplessly as Isabel ran out of the gym, alone.

By the time Avery got to the locker room, Isabel was
dressed and on her way out the door. Avery stuffed her
clothes in her bag and, still in her practice T-shirt and shorts,
ran down the hallway and outside the building after her.
Charlotte was in front of the school looking very confused.

"What's going on, Ave? Izzy ran by me and didn't even
say hello."

"She didn't make the exhibition team. Come on!" Avery
told Charlotte, waving her on. "Let's go after her." They took
off down the street after Isabel.

"I see her! She's just up there at the light," Charlotte puffed,
racing to keep up with Avery. "You must be freezing!"

"Not yet." Avery turned back to Charlotte, running at full
speed behind her. "What were you . . . still doing at school . . .
anyway?" Avery panted as she ran.

"Library. Ms. R . . . just approved . . . my book . . . report . . .
topic. And working on my . . ." Charlotte was desperately trying
to catch her breath. "Math project!"

"There!" Avery pointed. "Let's grab her!"

They sprinted ahead. Avery grabbed one of Isabel's arms
and Charlotte caught on to the other.

"Izzy," Avery said, gulping air as she caught her breath,
"I'm really sorry about the team."

"Forget it, okay?" Isabel replied, struggling to loosen her
friends' grips. "I don't care."

"Come on, Izzy, we're going to Montoya's. We all need a
hot chocolate," Charlotte told her.

"I just want to go home. Please let me go." Isabel wouldn't look at her friends.

"Only five of us made the team and we've been playing for years," Avery said. "You just started again, with your bad knee and everything."

"I know. It doesn't matter. I really have to go." Isabel yanked her arms back, but Charlotte immediately put a hand on her arm again, this time more softly.

"It *does* matter," Charlotte insisted. "We know you really wanted to play tomorrow night."

"Well, I did," Isabel said slowly. "I really wanted to tape the news segment from TV and send it to my dad."

Avery and Charlotte nodded. Isabel's dad was in Detroit, where he was running the family's accounting business while Mrs. Martinez was treated by her doctors in Boston. He came to visit as often as he could, but it was never enough. Avery knew exactly how Isabel felt. She wanted to send a video to her dad, too. She loved playing one-on-one with him in the driveway of his place in Colorado.

The overhead streetlights blinked on, and the three friends could see one another clearly. Avery was shivering in a gust of winter wind, and Isabel's long dark hair was blowing around her face.

"I know! Why don't we tape one of your upcoming games?" Charlotte suggested. "I could ask Chelsea Briggs to help us."

"Really? Do you think Chelsea would do that?" A touch of hope brightened Isabel's face.

Charlotte grabbed her friend hard. "I know she will. Chelsea loves anything to do with photography and video. We'll tape the whole game and then edit it down and add music and whatever else we want."

"That's a great idea. Thanks, you guys are the best." Isabel's face brightened. "But could you let me go now? I'm starting to feel like a criminal."

"No!" Avery yelled, latching on to Isabel's arm again. "We won't let you go until we're at Montoya's!"

The girls laughed into the cold air and raced down the street, holding on to Isabel's arms all the way across the park. The three of them ran until they were out of breath and giggling hysterically.

"BSG rocks!" Avery shouted. "And I'm not even cold!"

An old woman in a black fur hat and coat shook her finger and yelled at them for running through the park. "You girls better watch out. Do you hear me? Be careful!"

"Don't worry," Isabel reassured the lady, "we're fine! Better than fine!"

Mad with a Capital M

Still giggling, the girls spilled into Montoya's and sat down at their usual table. It was warm and bright and smelled of chocolate and coffee, honey, and pastries. Nick's older sister Fabiana brought over their hot chocolates. All the BSG loved Fabiana. Even though she was a junior in high school and had the lead role in *My Fair Lady*, Fabiana was never too busy to cover shifts at Montoya's or talk with the girls, and she always did everything with such style. She'd topped off their drinks with mounds of whipped cream and sprinkled on shaved chocolate and a touch of cinnamon.

Isabel felt so at home here. She loved the color of the sky blue walls that month to month displayed a local artist's photos or paintings. As Isabel sipped her hot chocolate, she felt her body relax for the first time all day. She looked up at her friends, grateful that they had made her come here.

"Your mom was right, Avery—chill time was in order," Isabel acknowledged. "Thanks for dragging me here."

"The pleasure was all ours!" Charlotte smiled after a big gulp of hot chocolate that left a whipped cream mustache. "I just hope we didn't scare that poor lady too badly."

"If anything, she's going to scare someone, dressed up like a bear!" Avery pronounced.

"Avery!" Isabel giggled into her hot chocolate.

"So, how'd your meeting go with Ms. R?" Isabel asked Charlotte.

"Great!" Charlotte answered. "She said my choice was fine, which is a relief because I've already written half of it."

Avery rolled her eyes jokingly. "*Half* already? You're the only person I know who gets her homework done early! I haven't even started mine. I can't concentrate at all this week. Maybe after the game. I'm psyched to write about MLK, though. Ms. R totally thought it was a great topic." Avery fake-shot a basket. "Two points for Abigail Adams!"

"I'll definitely be at the game, and Maeve's going too," Charlotte announced. "Are you going, Isabel?" she asked carefully, in case Isabel was still feeling sensitive about it.

Isabel smiled. "Of course! I wouldn't miss it. I have to support my team."

"What about Katani?" Avery asked.

"I don't know. I haven't really talked to her lately. Have you?" Isabel asked.

"Not really. She hasn't been at lunch for two days," Charlotte added. "It's like she's disappeared."

"Maybe the chill police should drag her down here to Montoya's, like you did to me!" Isabel laughed.

"Chill police—I like that," Avery smiled as she slurped some of her drink.

"What about you, Izzy? What happened with your idea of illustrating a myth?" Charlotte asked, spooning up the last bit of gooey chocolate at the bottom of her glass.

"Ms. R said she loved the idea. Big sigh of relief to that!" Isabel lifted her cup in a toast. "She thought it was a really creative approach to the book report idea." Isabel blushed a little when she told her friends, but couldn't wait to start painting the illustrations of Icarus.

"That's so great," Charlotte added.

The door to Montoya's opened and in walked Yurt and Dillon. The boys waved and headed toward the girls, who scooted over to make room for them.

"We need our chocolate fix, too," Dillon said.

"Especially this week," Avery agreed. "We're all in a state of total system overload!"

"How'd it go with Ms. R?" Charlotte asked the boys.

"Ms. R rejected my favorite book, *Smackdown at the WWE*. I am massively depressed," Yurt complained.

"What'd she say?" Avery asked.

"She said I should write about something like *A Wrinkle in Time*. Def not my thing." Yurt groaned. "Like I even understand that crazy story. Now I have to read an entire book *and* write a paper on it. I prefer politics." With that, the Yurt-meister popped a piece of Charlotte's cookie in his mouth.

"Don't worry, bro. Just hire Betsy Fitzgerald and you'll get a B or better," Dillon said. "You know I convinced Maeve to use her too."

"You did?" Avery blurted. "I mean, did she?"

"I think so, why not?" Dillon said. "Betsy's like some kind of tutoring genius. Now my paper is like something Nobel Prize winner Char here would write."

Uh-oh, Isabel thought. Why didn't Maeve talk to them

about this first? She was hiring Katani's rival. They all knew how competitive Katani was and how much this contest meant to her. The BSG looked at one another. Each of them knew what the others were thinking. Katani was going to be mad with a capital M.

Part Two
All's Fair in Basketball and Business

CHAPTER

11

Just Like Romeo and Juliet

Maeve raced down the hallway with a fresh bag of Swedish Fish tucked in her backpack. She almost ran right into Charlotte, who was just leaving the library.

"Are they closing?" she panted, out of breath.

"Pretty soon, I think. What's the rush?" asked Charlotte.

"I have to do some research, you know, for the English paper," Maeve rambled anxiously. *Why am I so nervous?* she thought. *It's not as if Charlotte could possibly guess I'm here because I'm working with Betsy.*

"Well, I better get started before they close!" she told Charlotte, a little too cheerfully. "I'll talk to you later, okay?"

"Sure," Charlotte said, giving her a funny look. "I'm going to meet some kids in my math class, anyway. I have to find out what they're doing with their project—before I meet with Betsy. She's talking to the Crow right now."

"Betsy Fitzgerald?" Maeve couldn't believe it.

"She's my partner for the math project, remember?"

"Oh, right, thanks to the Crow." Maeve could have told Charlotte right then. She could have told her that she'd just decided impulsively to call Betsy because she was desperate for some help and everyone else was so busy this week. Maybe she could trust Charlotte, who was always so sensible, to put things in perspective. But when she opened her mouth to say something, Charlotte was already turning away.

"Good luck!" Charlotte called, and disappeared down the hallway.

Maeve sighed unhappily. She'd just have to find some other time to tell them . . . later. She stepped inside the library and scanned the large room for Ms. Curtis. Although the school library was not on Maeve's list of top-ten places to hang out, Ms. Curtis the librarian was definitely one of her top-ten favorite teachers. She was really good at helping Maeve figure out ways to deal with her dyslexia without making her feel dumb.

"Well hello, Maeve!" Ms. Curtis greeted her, suddenly appearing behind the giant check-out desk. "The library is closing in fifteen minutes. Can I help you with something?"

"Um, yes," Maeve said, fumbling to remember what Betsy told her to ask for. "I'm doing a book report . . . so . . . I need to find some books, I guess. On *Romeo and Juliet*."

"Of course. Are you writing about the Shakespeare play?"

"Not exactly. I'm sort of doing my own interpretation of *Romeo and Juliet* based on the movie version. You know, the one with Leonardo Dicaprio. He's my favorite Romeo."

The librarian smiled. "Come on, then. Let's see what we can find." Ms. Curtis typed a search for *Romeo and Juliet* into the library catalog. She scrolled down the screen, reading through the list with Maeve.

"Now I have an important tip for your bibliography." She brought a stack of index cards over and showed Maeve how to write down all the information she needed.

"I can do this, no problem," Maeve said. For once, she actually felt excited about writing. Her book report was going to be so romantic and exciting! "Is it all right if I stay for a few more minutes?"

"Sure. I'm glad to see you're making progress."

Maeve did exactly what Betsy told her to do, typing all the information from her cards into her laptop. She had her bibliography completed before she even wrote her paper. Maeve was thrilled. For the first time in her life she felt like she had a firm handle on a school project. Betsy was worth every cent! After all, she was the one who'd walked Maeve through every step of the way.

Just as Maeve started to pack up her bag, Ms. Curtis came over and handed her a copy of William Shakespeare's *Romeo and Juliet*. "I thought you might want to read some of this—the original."

"I would," Maeve said confidently. She was surprising herself!

Maeve checked the book out and thanked Ms. Curtis for her help.

"Let me know what you think of the play."

"Oh, I will," Maeve promised the librarian. "If it's anything like the movie, I'm sure it's simply to *die* for!"

While she was waiting in the school lobby for her mother to pick her up for her hip-hop class, Maeve opened the library copy of *Romeo and Juliet* and started reading. Maeve thought she was reading another language. She flipped ahead to the first scene between Romeo and Juliet and imagined herself talking to Leonardo in the scene where the lovers have their first fated kiss. She read Romeo's line out loud: "Thus from my lips, by yours, my sin is purged." Maeve breathed in, her heart aching, and read Juliet's response: "Then have my lips the sin that they have took." And Romeo's: "Sin from my lips? O trespass sweetly urged! Give me my sin again." Just as fabulously romantic as the movie, Maeve concluded. Maybe reading Shakespeare wasn't completely snooze-inducing after all. Plus, she thought maybe Shakespeare was dyslexic. His spelling was totally weird.

Go Fly a Kite

"Sorry I'm a little late," Katani apologized as she rushed through Mr. Sherman's door. "I wanted to make some corrections to my plan before I showed it to you."

The Crow wrinkled his brow and looked at Katani for a few long seconds before he said, "You can't afford to be late, Katani. If this were a real business meeting, you would have already made a bad impression."

Katani nodded and mumbled she was sorry again, that it was a crazy week. Of course he was right, she should have been more aware of the time. There just didn't seem to be enough hours to do everything. *What's happening to the Kgirl?* Katani felt she didn't even recognize herself these days.

Mr. Sherman picked up her smartly laid out budget and took his time going over her figures, occasionally marking the page. After a few minutes he sat back and said, "I'm impressed, Katani. You know, I never would have dreamed of running a company at your age—or my age, as a matter of fact!" He laughed. "In any case, you've done a fine job. I've made a few comments that we can go over now."

He proceeded to go over each line item and made a few suggestions on the overall company goal and future investment plan. The more they talked, the more excited Katani was about the project and her business. It was all starting to become real. She was actually going to do this!

"Thanks, Mr. Sherman. This has been very helpful," Katani told him. Maybe the Crow wasn't really that bad of a guy, she thought. She'd have to tell Maeve not to be so hard on her friend's least-favorite teacher.

"I'm here to help," Mr. Sherman responded, "but I have to say again, I would have preferred you worked on the Egyptian math project with Reggie."

Oops, cancel previous opinion, Katani thought. "Yeah, me too," she answered with irritation. She still couldn't believe that Reggie had dropped her as a partner. Who did he think he was, anyway?

Katani heard footsteps and glanced up to see Math Boy standing between her and their math teacher.

"Sorry . . . I . . . just . . . well . . . ," he mumbled, and looked sheepishly over at Katani.

Was the great Math Boy making like things were just fine and groovy now? He hadn't even responded to her note! No way was she going to acknowledge his presence.

"How's the project going, Reggie?" Mr. Sherman asked.

"Great . . . I just wanted to run a couple things by you," he explained, and then dropped some papers on Mr. Sherman's desk. "I guess I kind of overreacted when you didn't show the other day, Katani. Sorry about that," he said, looking down at Katani's shoes. "Thanks for the note."

Katani gathered her papers together and rose like Cleopatra from her throne. With every ounce of confidence she could muster, she stood tall and mighty and said, "Excuse me, Mr. Sherman, I have another very important date," and she swept out of the room.

CHAPTER
12
Storm Clouds

Snapping her fingers in the air and shaking her head from side to side, Katani stomped her way toward the school lobby. As if Reggie apologizing would make them friends again, she fumed. Clearly Math Boy was clueless. He had absolutely no idea what she was going through this week!

As she stormed outside to wait for Mrs. Fields, she almost crashed right into Betsy Fitzgerald, the last person on earth she wanted to see. And wouldn't you know it, Betsy was carrying a black leather briefcase. Grudgingly, Katani had to admit that Betsy looked scarily professional.

"Well, I'm running into all the BSG today!" Betsy said a bit smugly. "Right after basketball with Avery and Isabel, I saw Charlotte for a minute to talk about our math project." Betsy paused. "And then of course, I have to talk to Maeve later about her project."

"Maeve?" Katani asked, confused.

"Oh, I'm tutoring Maeve to help her with math and her English paper," Betsy proudly explained. "I have to say, everyone is pretty psyched with my service right now. Just ask Maeve and Dillon. And, okay, Billy Trentini asked me for help too."

Billy Trentini, too. Betsy's business was doing so awesomely well Katani wanted to scream. But Maeve! Maeve hadn't even told Katani that she'd hired Betsy! Where was the loyalty? Did the other BSG know too? Katani felt a major meltdown coming on. She had to get away from Betsy Fitzgerald, "business consultant to the stars."

But Betsy followed her. "I've also worked with Jolene—"

Before Betsy could rattle more names off her list, Katani headed toward the parking lot, mumbling, "I have to find my grandmother." She just couldn't take another minute of Betsy Fitzgerald.

As Katani crossed the lot to meet Mrs. Fields, she caught a glimpse of herself in a car window, shivering and hunched inside her long, wool coat. She didn't even look like herself. "Things better change, and soon," she whispered.

Katani could hear that clock ticking inside her head again. Four days to go. She had to knit twenty scarves (well, fourteen really, counting Mrs. Martinez's three and the three Katani had already finished), finalize the contest application, work through the sales plan, revise the financial budget, take pictures of the final product, and on top of all that, do two school projects! And . . . she hadn't even started writing her English paper.

She quickened her pace and tried to swallow the lump in her throat. Betsy was so far ahead of her—her tutoring business was already going full swing—and she had the same school schedule as Katani. Betsy was on the basketball team, too. How did she manage it all? Katani had to succeed; she absolutely had to. *Be your own cheerleader,* her mother always said. She had to pull things together, and fast!

Yellow Fever

Thrilled about her session with Ms. Curtis in the library, Maeve practically skipped to the school parking lot while she rummaged through her bag of red, yellow, green, and orange Swedish Fish. She chose a yellow. She *felt* yellow today— hippie-dippy happy yellow. The first bite of fish was so sweet and chewy, it immediately filled her with a bright and flowery sun-yellow feeling. She tried to chew slowly to make each one last longer, but it was too hard. She popped two more yellows into her mouth as she almost skipped right into Katani.

"How could you do that to me?" Katani blurted.

Maeve took one look at Katani's furious face and knew exactly what she was talking about. All of a sudden, Maeve's happy yellow feelings burst like a balloon, and she tried to respond.

"Look, Katani, I meant to tell you, but—" Suddenly Maeve started coughing. Half a yellow fish stuck in her throat. Just as she finally gulped down the sticky yellow glob, her mother pulled up beside the girls.

"Let's get going, Maeve. We're late! Your dance class started ten minutes ago." Maeve's mother sounded a little impatient, even as she waved at Katani.

"Uh . . . we'll talk later, okay?" Maeve promised Katani as she got in the car. When she closed the door, she hung her head. Her hippie-dippy yellow mood had turned to gruesome gray. Maeve had known Katani wouldn't like her working with Betsy, but she hadn't expected that it would feel quite this awful—that Katani would be this mad. Maeve had to talk to someone. Her mother was looking at her, eyebrow raised, waiting for her to say something.

"Maeve?" her mother asked. "Is everything okay between you and Katani?"

That was all it took. Maeve poured out the whole sad story, confessing to her mom all the gory details. "What should I do?" she finally asked in despair.

"You have to talk to her as soon as possible and try to explain," her mother said sensibly. "She feels like you betrayed her."

"That's what I thought," Maeve said, and sighed tragically.

"Katani sounds like she's got a lot going on this week. Maybe she could use some help too," her mother suggested.

"How could someone like me possibly help someone like Katani? I mean, she's like the ace student, a math whiz and everything."

"Just being there for her as a friend will help a lot."

A Million Things to Do
Charlotte's Journal

> *Wed. night, 7:50 p.m.*
> *We had the best time at Montoya's this afternoon. Avery and I dragged Isabel (who didn't make the exhibition b-ball team) all the way through the park. We were laughing so much, it hurt. My sides still ache! It made me think that we need to have a Tower sleepover SOON! I'm going to schedule one as soon as we all have time. Did time suddenly speed up or what?*
>
> *On the Nick front, I'm going to take Sophie's advice. As much as I want to go to the Omni movie, I have to finish these projects first or I'll be distracted and won't have a good time. I know that about me. But I'm so nervous about telling Nick I need to postpone our non-date-date. I wish I knew what he was thinking.*

I have to get back to work now. Betsy and I have a "power meeting" (that's what she called it) after school tomorrow. We have to crank out the "Million Project." We're going to estimate how long it would take to do something a million times (baking cookies, running three miles, watching a movie) and then estimate all sorts of different equations, games, etc.

In the meantime, I love writing about Anne of Green Gables. I decided to focus on the power of communication for my topic. I sure hope Katani doesn't stop talking to Maeve when she finds out about Betsy—like Anne did to Gilbert! Anne was so stubborn, she wouldn't even admit that she wasn't mad at Gilbert anymore until the end! Okay, okay. Back to work right now, Charlotte Ramsey.

Avery's Blog:

I love the amazing rock-climbing experiences you guys posted! Totally cool. Thanks for contributing. The rest of you—get out there and rock on this week!

Martin Luther King says the time is always right to do what is right! Go, MLK. I'm writing my English paper on him. Well, I haven't started yet, but I will. I talked to my grandmother and she told me some cool stuff about him. Like he was a student at Boston University during the 1950s! Maybe I'll post my report here so you can all read about what a truly amazing person he was. Please vote: YES to post it, or NO. I'm too excited about the game tomorrow night to start it now, though. Less than twenty-four hours to go before game-time! Remember, I'll be looking for a major wave when I'm on the court.

The time is right for me to go fill up on carbs! Scott

just baked an apple pie — and he made homemade ice cream
to go with. What are Mom and I going to do when he goes
to college?

   Later! Wish us luck!

Making a Splash

"*Vámanos*! Go start your project!" Mrs. Martinez told Isabel, laughing. "I will do the dishes. I feel very healthy tonight. Perhaps I will even train for the Boston Marathon." She winked at her daughter. "And I bought some new watercolor paper from the art store," she revealed with a big smile. Mrs. Martinez was almost as excited as Isabel that the myth idea had been approved by Ms. R.

"Oh, thank you, Mama!" Isabel exclaimed. Before she left for school that morning, Isabel had told her mother watercolors would be the best medium for her illustrations. "Did you walk to the store by yourself?"

She nodded. "I wanted to surprise all of you."

"You bought it before Ms. R said the project was okay?" Isabel tilted her head toward her mother.

"*Si, bonita*. I knew such a wonderful idea would not get turned down by such a teacher as Ms. Rodriguez."

Isabel hugged her mother tight. Then she went into the dining room and spread her paper and paints out on the table. She had done quick sketches of the story, but now she was eager to start drawing on the big, thick, cottony sheets of paper her mother had bought. First she'd sketch, and then she'd paint. She hoped everyone would fall in love with the story of Icarus, like she had.

On the first page she drew Icarus and his father Daedalus imprisoned in the tower of Crete by King Minos. They were looking out the tower window at the sea and sky beyond.

She'd use deep blue so the sea would mirror the sky, and she'd add a tinge of watery green to the ocean and swirls of cloud to the sky. The sun would be a shimmering ball with great white birds flying around it. At the bottom of the page she printed Daedalus saying, "Minos may control the land and the sea, but not the regions of the air. I will try that way."

For the next page, she drew Daedalus and Icarus gathering feathers to make wings. In the following scene, she showed Daedalus fastening the beautiful wings onto his son and then himself, the smallest feathers glued with candle wax and the larger ones sewn with thread.

Isabel stepped back to observe her sketches. It was so much easier to say what she wanted to say with images rather than words! Staring at the page where Icarus was flying too close to the sun, she'd make drops of wax melting from his wings. In the distance his father would be calling his name. But it would be too late! Poor, brave Icarus would fall into the sea.

If that's not dramatic enough even for Maeve, I don't know what is, Isabel thought with a smile. But the story of ambitious Icarus reminded her of a certain other BSG too—one with more ambition than any girl she knew. Looking at her sketch, Isabel gulped. Could Katani really do everything on her own . . . or would she end up all wet?

13

Pinkie-swear Secret

Katani's parents were out and her grandmother was working on the school budget, so everyone was having a grab bag dinner. Katani wolfed down Patrice's leftover special homemade pizza with sundried tomatoes, kalamata olives, and ricotta and mozzarella cheese. Grandma Ruby, who was munching on a Caesar salad at the table, occasionally glanced over at Katani in that all-knowing way. Katani could tell that her grandmother had sensed something was wrong between her and Maeve the minute she picked up Katani at school. Katani wished she could talk to her grandmother about it, but she was afraid she'd blurt out the whole story about the contest and everything.

Kelley was also under Grandma Ruby's watchful eye. When their grandmother asked how Kelley's afternoon was, Kelley pretended to zip her lips shut with her fingers and wouldn't say a word. Then she gave Katani the pinkie-swear shake under the table.

"Well, Patrice, I hope you can tell me something about your day," Grandma Ruby said pointedly, while she gave

Katani her "I AM THE PRINCIPAL" look. The one that said, "I'm watching you, and I know something is up, and you better tell me before the trouble starts." Katani hated that look.

Thank goodness Patrice went on about how busy she was with basketball and how they were definitely going to make the play-offs this year. On top of that, Patrice announced that she had Student Council, the Honor Society, and a major math test tomorrow.

Katani blocked her sister out. In her mind she envisioned Patrice floating away on a puffy cloud. Bye-bye, she waved. She was so tired of Patrice always making everything look so easy and doing everything just right.

Patrice grabbed a few brownies and called "Gotta go!" on her way out the door to her library meeting. As soon as she was gone, Grandma Ruby went upstairs to work in her study, but said that she wanted to have a talk with Katani later. *What's that about?* Katani thought. *Is she going to try to get me to tell her the whole story now?* A tiny part of Katani acknowledged it might be a relief to tell someone who cared about her how hard everything had become lately.

She looked over at Kelley, who was finishing her favorite pudding. "I'm busy, very very busy, Katani," Kelley told her with an extremely serious expression. "I need time by myself right now. I'm very, very busy." As she watched her sister bound up the stairs, Katani was puzzled. Usually, Kelley wanted to talk to Katani about everything. But she decided to take advantage of the quiet to start rereading *Let the Circle Be Unbroken*.

However, as soon as she opened the book, all she could think about was all the things that were bothering her. Why would Maeve use Betsy's tutoring business? It really was a complete betrayal, as far as Katani was concerned. *Well, fine. If Maeve cares so little about loyalty between friends, then I'm going to just stop caring too.* Then Katani thought of Reggie acting so dense and Mr. Sherman telling her that if their meeting that afternoon had been a real business meeting, she wouldn't have made a good impression being late. Why couldn't she seem to get anything right? she asked herself. *Maybe I'm just not cut out to be a business owner after all.*

Worse, the scarves she had to knit loomed over her. The idea of them was like a weight pressing into her shoulders. With a big sigh, she put down the book and took up the scarf she was halfway through knitting.

Suddenly Kelley ran in and plopped herself down right next to Katani. "You're busy, aren't you, Katani? Busy, busy, busy like a bee."

"Yes, Kelley." Katani tried to be patient. After all, a minute ago she had wanted her sister's company.

"You're *too* busy!" Kelley announced, sidling up close to Katani. "So I helped knit some scarves."

"What?" Katani was now exasperated.

"Close your eyes. Don't peek, Katani. Promise?"

"Promise."

"Okay, open."

Katani stared at three pink mohair scarves exactly like the ones she was knitting for the contest. "Where did you get these?" she asked, astounded.

"I made them. Remember? You taught me how! It's easy-peasy. See, I've been busy, busy, busy like a bee too."

Katani's mouth opened, and she stared at her sister. "You made these for me?"

"I saw all your yarn."

The stitches were a bit loose, but Katani had to admit the

scarves were impressive for someone who'd just learned how to knit.

"Thank you," Katani said, her eyes filling. She couldn't believe Kelley had really done this for *her*. She reached her arms around Kelley, and Kelley let her hold on for a moment. Katani knew that was a big deal for her sister, who really didn't like to be touched.

Suddenly, Kelley flung herself away from Katani. "They're for our pinkie-swear secret," she whispered dramatically. "Now I'm going to knit little scarves for Mr. Bear. Pink mohair Mr. Bear scarves."

"Pink ones for Mr. Bear?" Katani asked, slowly putting together what Kelley was saying.

"Yes. He wants pink, don't you, Mr. Bear?" Kelley said as she gave her bear a squeeze.

For the first time, Katani realized that Kelley was really serious about entering the contest with her. No way could that happen. Kelley as her business partner? Total disaster! Kelley always meant well, but Katani just knew that if she got involved in her project it would ruin *everything*. But she knew better than to upset Kelley right now, so she kept her mouth shut.

"Did you find the yarn behind my sewing curtain?" Katani asked.

Kelley nodded. "For the pinkie-swear secret."

"Why don't you start on Mr. Bear's scarves?" Katani tried to keep her voice level, but she thought she was an inch away from losing it. She turned back to the scarf she was knitting so she could focus on something and get one more scarf done, or at least well under way.

"All right, Kgirl," Kelley said. "I'm a Kgirl, too! Katani and Kelley. K names, K girls."

Just as Katani began to count slowly to herself, the door-bell rang.

Kelley jumped up. "Who's that? Who's here, Katani? Someone must know about our secret!"

She yanked the bedspread down over the scarves. The bell rang a second time.

"Don't let them in. No one can come in here. Right, Katani?"

"It's okay, Kelley. Don't worry. Grandma Ruby will get the door."

A couple minutes later, Grandma Ruby opened the door to Katani and Kelley's bedroom. "Maeve's here, Katani."

"Maeve?" Katani stopped knitting.

"Maeve!" Kelley shouted. "Maeve's here, Katani! We can't tell her about the pinkie-swear secret!"

Katani wouldn't even look at Grandma Ruby. She wished her grandmother weren't so smart about every little thing. It was starting to get on her nerves.

"Let's all go down and say hello to Maeve and then I have something special I want to show you in my study, Kelley," said Grandma Ruby, her eyes never leaving Katani's.

"Maeve!" Kelley shouted, and ran down the stairs. She clapped her hands when she saw Maeve.

"Hi, Kelley!" Maeve gave Kelley a wave and a big smile. All the BSG were supportive and friendly to Kelley.

Grandma Ruby encouraged Kelley to follow her upstairs, promising her a treat, and Maeve and Katani were left standing on opposite sides of the kitchen, glancing at each other. The only sound was the refrigerator humming between them. Katani, arms folded, watched Maeve shifting her feet side to side and resisted the urge to say, "Well, how does it feel to betray your friend?"

Finally Maeve took a deep breath and tucked some loose strands of curly red hair behind her ear. "I'm soooo sorry about this whole Betsy mess. I really am, Katani. It's just, I know you never need any help with your homework, but I *really, really* do. Writing is so hard for me. I never know where to begin and then I get all messed up and it's just a totally bad, awful, horrible scene.

"And this week is crazy, like a total overload. My dad's in New York, my mom has a major project, my tutor, Matt, is out of town, and the BSG are all too busy with their own projects to help me. I know Betsy's entering your contest, but she's a really good tutor . . . and the only one I could get on such short notice. I mean, she's actually pretty cool when you talk to her. And it feels so awesome to actually know what I'm doing on a big project!" Maeve digressed. "Please don't be mad at me, Katani." Maeve looked up at her friend with pleading eyes.

Katani understood that Maeve felt awful, and then she thought of everything that had gone wrong with her day, and it was just too much. Katani burst out crying right there in the middle of the kitchen.

Maeve's mouth dropped open, her eyes widened, and she jumped back. She'd never seen Katani cry so hard before . . . ever. The Kgirl was always composed and together. Now Katani covered her face with her hands, her whole body shaking. Maeve went to her friend and put a comforting arm around her shoulders.

"Please don't cry, Katani. It's okay. I didn't mean to make you more upset. Don't worry, things will be fine. I promise I won't use Betsy anymore. Please don't cry!"

Katani's chest heaved in and out until she caught her breath. Then she wiped her face with a kitchen cloth. "It's not

Betsy," she sniffled. "It's everything!" And then she let out one final sob.

"When in doubt, call a BSG. You should know that!" Maeve smiled at her friend. "My dad sometimes makes tea for me when I'm upset. You want some?"

Katani gave her a small smile. "Grandma Ruby does that too."

Katani directed Maeve to the tea bags and mugs. Katani splashed cold water on her face while Maeve brewed the Chai tea. As she handed Katani her cup, she said, "What's up? What's going on with you? Talk to Auntie Maeve."

Katani snorted. "Ugh. Everything's such a total mess, I don't even know where to start."

"The beginning?"

"I guess that's as good a place as any." Katani smiled and took a sip of tea. "I told you about Whitney from High Hopes. I just knew all she wanted was information about the contest. That's when it started." Once she started, Katani couldn't stop. It felt so good to spill everything.

"Then I forgot to bring the application for Pony Camp home that day, so Kelley and I probably won't be able to go because we don't go back there for over a week and the camp fills up really fast. Then we have so much work this week at school, it's not fair. Why does it all have to come now? Ms. R approved my *Let the Circle Be Unbroken* idea, but I haven't even started the paper yet." With a hint of a smile, Katani added, "I did find a place to sell my scarves. Guess where?"

"Where?" Maeve sipped her tea and leaned forward.

"Well, they're pink mohair. Pink with heart beads on the ends."

"Think Pink!? Wow, Katani!" Maeve exclaimed. "Only

my absolute favorite store in the entire universe!"

"Ms. Pink's going to display them in the window, and a portion of the sales will go to support breast cancer research. My only problem is that I have to knit all the scarves by Sunday. Isabel's mother is knitting three of them for me, and I've finished three, but I still have to do fourteen more." Katani closed her eyes. "That's the deal. I don't know how I'm going to do it on top of everything else!"

Maeve started pacing the kitchen. "That's too much knitting," she said. "You might collapse or something."

Katani nodded. "Kelley knitted three, too, but the stitches are too loose and I don't think I can use them."

"That was sweet of her and Mrs. Martinez."

"Yeah. But Isabel doesn't know that her mom is helping me, so you can't tell her, okay? I just want to make sure I can really do this before it becomes a huge deal for everyone."

Maeve nodded.

Katani sighed and went on. "And the other thing is, while I was talking to Ms. Pink, I totally lost track of time and I was late to meet Math Boy. We were supposed to talk about our math project. Reggie was so mad, he told Mr. Sherman he didn't want to work with me anymore."

"No way!"

"It worked out because Mr. Sherman said I could use my budget plan, but I still can't believe that Reggie dumped me."

"That *was* kind of harsh. I mean, everyone's allowed to make a mistake on occasion . . . even you," Maeve agreed.

"And Kelley thinks she's going to enter the contest too. She's making pink scarves for Mr. Bear just like my scarves. I have to tell her this is *my* thing, but I have to be super careful. You know Kelley." Katani shook her head.

Maeve smiled. "She just wants to help."

"That's one way to put it." Katani took a big gulp of her tea, which was lukewarm by now. "And I haven't been able to talk to the BSG about anything because I've been too busy and stressed out."

"Hmmm. That's sure a lot to do by yourself, Katani. I can't help you with any of the school stuff, but I think I have a good idea for your scarves," Maeve said. Her eyes were bright and twinkling.

They heard Katani's grandmother humming as she came down the stairs.

Maeve asked quickly, "Who all knows about the contest?"

"The BSG, Kelley, some of the girls in my horseback riding class, and a few people at school."

"OK, meet me at Irving's after school tomorrow and bring all your yarn," Maeve instructed her. "I know some people who can help you."

"Okay. But, Maeve—"

"Yeah?"

"This is just between us, right? You won't tell any of the other BSG? I'd be really embarrassed if they knew what a mess I'm in."

Mrs. Fields peeked her head into the kitchen. "Tell me when, Maeve."

"It's pretty late. I should probably go now," Maeve answered, looking at Katani.

"I'll go warm up the car. Kelley's upstairs waiting for you, Katani."

When Mrs. Fields had left the kitchen, Maeve told her friend, "Okay, pinkie-swear . . . just between us. And you should really go to bed, Katani. Everything will be better in the morning, believe me. Maevelicious to the rescue!" she said as she pumped her hand in the air.

"Thanks, Maeve." Katani smiled at her dramatic friend.

Even though she was totally exhausted, Katani felt so much better about everything. Maeve might not be the best student in the world, but she was an outstanding friend. Nothing had actually changed as far as all the stuff she had to do, but after talking to Maeve, she felt 110 percent lighter, like an elephant had just flown off her chest.

"Kelley!" she called up the stairs. "Do you want me to read some fairy tales before we go to bed?"

"Yes, yes, yes!" Kelley danced down the hallway. "I love 'The Princess and the Pea, Pea, Pea'!"

Tonight Katani needed a happily-ever-after ending.

14

The Knitwits to the Rescue

Charlotte stared at the second hand speeding around and around the face of her watch. She had been waiting until the end of Ms. R's after-school prep session to talk to Nick. *Okay, no more stalling,* Charlotte thought as she saw him get up from his desk. *I have to do this now.*

"Hey, Nick," she said in a rushed voice. "I think we should postpone Saturday. I have so much work to do this week."

"Yeah, that's cool. I'm totally swamped with all these projects—math and English, plus I have all this extra lab work for science." Charlotte thought Nick actually seemed relieved. "And there's the bakery. Everyone's busy this week, not just me."

"Way too busy," Charlotte agreed. "Isn't this supposed to be hibernation season?"

Nick laughed. "Let's just go on another Saturday."

"Sounds good," Charlotte said. That was easy. Was it too easy? He still hadn't called it a date. Why was all this so hard to figure out? Either way, she would definitely have to IM the BSG tonight and let them know the non-date-date was postponed for now.

"I guess I better go now. I have to work later," Nick said. "Are you walking home?"

"I am." Charlotte packed up her papers, and the two of them walked down the hall together.

Just as they were leaving, Chelsea Briggs came flying out of the darkroom with something under her arm. She was carrying it like it was made of precious gems.

Charlotte said hi and asked, "Were you printing something special?"

A smile spread across Chelsea's face like a half moon and she clutched the book to her chest. "I could show you if you want."

"Okay," Nick said. "Let's go to the bakery. I've got to work in a little while."

"Any excuse to have a hot chocolate and a cookie," Charlotte reasoned.

"I'm ready," Chelsea said. She seemed to walk with a bounce in her step.

Outside, tiny flakes of snow were blowing this way and that in the wind. Charlotte opened her mouth and caught one on her tongue and began to spin around. Chelsea joined in as Nick grabbed some in his fist and flung them in the air. Snow dances weren't exactly his thing.

"Cool," he said. "Maybe we'll have a snow day tomorrow."

When they arrived at Montoya's, Nick noted, "Looks like we have the whole place to ourselves."

"I've never seen it this empty," Chelsea commented.

"Maybe I won't have to work after all," Nick said. "Where should we sit?"

Chelsea pointed to a table by the window so they could watch the flakes. The girls gave Nick some money for their drinks and chocolate pistachio biscotti just out of the oven.

When he brought the drinks and treats over, Chelsea reached for a biscotti, then changed her mind. "Want to split one, Charlotte?" she asked.

"Sure!" Charlotte agreed. She wanted to support Chelsea, who had been on this serious health kick since the class trip to Lake Rescue last fall.

Chelsea laid her treasure on the table. "It's a travel scrapbook for my mom—for her birthday. We've gone a lot of places together."

She slowly turned the pages covered with cool photos and souvenirs like ticket stubs and brochures, all labeled with captions and entries telling about each place they visited.

"Wow, Chels, you've been to so many states!" Nick said. "I can't wait to go on a road trip."

"My mom loves traveling. She'll go somewhere just to look at the houses and buildings. I guess that's why she's a real estate agent." She pointed to a picture of the Sears Tower. "Like this is from a boat tour of Chicago's architecture. We could see the whole city from the water. Then we went to the Frank Lloyd Wright Museum. My mom was crazy for that."

Chelsea pointed and turned the page. "And here's the house Ernest Hemingway grew up in."

"He went from Illinois to Paris—it's like the reverse of my life!" Charlotte laughed. "I love seeing where writers lived. It's really inspiring."

"I think so too." Chelsea turned the page. "And here's my mom eating shark bites in Tampa. I tried them, too. They tasted like tough chicken."

"I tried antelope and ostrich in Africa," Charlotte said. "And I tasted my dad's bush rat."

"You ate rat?" Chelsea exclaimed. "Ew! That's one thing I'd never try."

"I swallowed a goldfish when I was little," Nick told them, "but it was an accident. My mom put it in a cup while she was cleaning out the bowl."

The girls didn't know whether to laugh or groan, so they did both.

"Are these redwoods?" Charlotte asked, pointing to a forest of the most magnificent tall trees.

Chelsea nodded. "In Northern California. They're amazing. I never felt so small in my life! I was like a squirrel beside those trees."

"Have you always taken pictures of the outdoors?" Nick asked.

"I always loved taking pictures of our trips so I could remember every detail. But it wasn't until we took that school trip to Lake Rescue that I really looked up close at nature and stuff. I didn't want to go up there at all, and then it turned out to be one of the best trips I've ever taken. I always learn so much when I go to a new place." Chelsea turned a few pages to show them a few photos of the black and white loons through a gray mist on Lake Rescue.

"You know, since Lake Rescue, I like being out more, and I'm so busy doing my photography. My mom's happy about that. That's why I'm giving her this book—I mean, besides her birthday. She was always trying to get me to exercise and eat better, and now I'm on *her* case about her sweet tooth!"

Charlotte nodded. She remembered how kids used to make fun of Chelsea by calling her "Chelsea Biggs." It wasn't until Lake Rescue that a lot of people started seeing Chelsea Briggs for who she was—a really great girl with a passion for photography.

"My mom always tells me, let food be your medicine and let medicine be your food. Some Greek guy said it," Nick told them.

"Hippocrates," Charlotte piped up. "He said it."

"Yeah, that's right," Nick replied. "It's what she tells me and Fabiana whenever we want to chow down the serious junk food, because good food is so important to her."

Chelsea nodded. "My mom says in other countries kids don't snack like they do here."

"It's true," Charlotte agreed. "From what I've seen, I mean. That's my favorite part of traveling—learning how people live and seeing how different they are. But it's funny because we're all so much the same, too. Take Shadya, my friend in Africa. Her family would roast a whole goat on their religious holidays. I couldn't exactly imagine roasting a goat on Corey Hill! But I can get into a big turkey dinner. And Sophie, my best friend in Paris. Even though I sent her a Red Sox cap, she cannot understand how anyone could watch a baseball game. She says it's so long and boring and what's the point. But she loves watching boring French movies."

Nick laughed. "I guess she's never seen Big Papi!" he joked, naming his favorite Red Sox player.

"All kids must like ice cream," Chelsea said definitively.

"And no kids like making their beds," Nick said. "Well, except maybe Katani."

"And probably Betsy, too," Charlotte added.

"I really wish we could make that travel website for kids," Nick exclaimed. "Kids could write about places they've gone and trade stories about all the crazy stuff that happens."

"And maybe they could post photos so we could really see these places," Charlotte added.

"Once we build the site!" Chelsea laughed.

"Oh, yeah, I forgot about that part!" Nick laughed too. Nobody had time to do anything this week, much less create a website.

What a Bunch of Knitwits

Katani walked with Maeve over to Irving's Toy and Card Shop, Maeve's favorite place to buy penny candy. "Katani, I am one hundred percent sure Mrs. Weiss can help you out," Maeve assured her. Mrs. Weiss, the friendly owner of Irving's, had a soft spot for Maeve. "You just have to trust me on this one." But she refused to say anything else about it. Instead, she asked about Math Boy. "Did you talk to Reggie at all today?"

"He said hi and I said hi. That was it." Katani shrugged. "I took your advice and got a good sleep last night. I feel a trillion times better—but I still have all these scarves to knit by Sunday! How am I ever going to manage?"

Maeve just smiled and walked ahead.

"You think that's funny?" Katani demanded as she quickened her pace. "You try it!"

The bell on the door to Irving's clanged when Maeve pushed it open. Katani liked Irving's too, because it had lots of cool stuff, and because the store had a sweet cinnamon scent like her grandmother's study, and because Mrs. Weiss always had a big stash of Swedish Fish. In Maeve's world, Swedish Fish were one of life's necessities, and on days like this, Katani had to agree.

No one else was in the store, so Maeve went straight to the register with Katani and her pink mohair yarn in tow and began to tell Mrs. Weiss all about Katani's tragic situation. As she explained the predicament Katani was in, Mrs. Weiss listened, occasionally nodding sympathetically.

Finally the proprietor of Irving's said, "Sounds like you bit off more than you could chew."

Maeve and Katani nodded at the same time. Mrs. Weiss had this reassuring way of making confusing things sound simple, and making you feel like you weren't the only person in the world with that problem.

"So, what do you think we should do?" Maeve winked at Mrs. Weiss.

With a warm smile, Mrs. Weiss asked Katani. "What do you need the most, Katani?"

Katani swallowed. "I really need some expert knitters to help with the scarves," she admitted, looking down, "but I don't know anyone else who could knit that much in just a few days. I mean I just can't walk into a store and ask for a bunch of random people to help me!"

Maeve knowingly glanced at Mrs. Weiss and asked, "What do you think—a job for the Knitwits?"

"None other," Mrs. Weiss agreed.

Katani frowned, very confused. Who were the *nitwits* and how were they supposed to help her? Was this some kind of joke? She had no time for jokes today.

"Um, who are—"

"Just a minute, girls," Mrs. Weiss interrupted her cheerfully. While she went to grab her hat and coat from the back room, Maeve put a finger to her lips and smiled mysteriously.

"All right, let's go!" Mrs. Weiss exclaimed, sweeping an eager Maeve and a very confused Katani out the door. She locked Irving's and hung a sign on the door that read BE BACK IN 20 MINUTES.

Katani felt silly carrying her bags of yarn as she tried to keep up with Mrs. Weiss, who, despite her age, walked ahead, fast and determined. "So, Mrs. Weiss," she started tentatively, "where *are* we going?"

"To see a very special group of friends," she told them. "The Knitwits. I told Maeve about them because they remind me of the BSG, only older. Much older."

"Why do they call themselves nitwits?" Katani asked, trying to be polite. *Who in their right mind would want to be known as a nitwit?* she wondered.

"Knitting," Mrs. Weiss answered, chuckling, and pointing to Katani's bags of yarn. "They all love knitting. Knitwits with a K."

Katani sighed with relief. "Oh, now I get it."

Maeve giggled and grabbed Katani's arm. "I told you she could help."

"The ladies put their money together and bought a brownstone so none of them would have to live alone as they got older. You'll get a kick out of them. They're feisty all right, real firecrackers. A group of five—like you girls," Mrs. Weiss explained.

"What are their names again?" Maeve asked.

Katani felt bewildered by all of this. Did she really want to let a group of little old ladies help her? What if they were really slow or they couldn't see? This could be another disaster, Katani worried.

"We're almost there now," Mrs. Weiss said. "Let me fill you in quickly. June is a retired army field nurse. She's very straightforward, a real live-wire. Sally used to be a social worker and she might go back to work after some time off— she's recently widowed. She's just lovely. They all are. Frances is a teacher at Somerville High. And Maeve, you'll be glad to meet Delilah, a former actress, and Natasha, who used to dance with the Boston Ballet. Now she's a yoga teacher.

They're all great fun. Very independent gals. Here we are."

Mrs. Weiss rang the bell on the cobalt blue door. "At the Bluebell House."

The House with the Blue Door

A woman with shimmering white hair pulled back into a loose bun answered the door. She was wearing black leggings and a purple sweater that reached to her knees. "Ethel, what a lovely surprise!" she said, and gave Mrs. Weiss a quick hug. She introduced herself as Frances to Katani and Maeve, glancing with a smile at Katani's two bags of pink mohair yarn.

"Come in everyone, please. Just in time for tea and my special home-baked cookies."

Katani heard someone playing piano as they followed Frances into a soft blue-colored room with ceilings so high the air seemed lighter and easier to breathe. Katani already felt better. There was something very soothing about Bluebell House. Maybe it was the sweet smell of cider wafting from the stove, or maybe the sky blue walls covered with paintings and family photographs. Or possibly it was the soft gray tapestries hung from the walls and the woven white rug covering the middle of the floor. All Katani knew was the house made her feel happy and relaxed. Books and magazines were stacked all around the room and there were beautiful crystal vases, colorful masks, a bronze statue of a woman stretching into a dance—there were so many wonderful things to take in!

One of the Knitwits was playing the piano while the others sat in a circle of comfortable chairs, sipping tea and eating chocolate cookies. When they saw the group, the ladies immediately stood and introduced themselves, shaking hands with the girls and chattering away. Right away the women reminded Katani of Grandma Ruby and Miss Pierce,

Charlotte's landlady. They might be old, but they were lovely and smart, and it seemed like they got to do whatever they wanted. Katani hoped to be just like them when she got older. Maybe all the BSG could buy a house together.

The Knitwits invited their guests to stay for tea. "Of course, thank you," said Mrs. Weiss, "but we are in a bit of a hurry. I have to be back at the store in ten minutes. After all, what if some poor soul came looking for Swedish Fish?" She winked at Maeve.

Then Mrs. Weiss turned to the Knitwits. "Let me tell you why we're here." She proceeded to tell them Katani's story. The women listened, nodding sympathetically, and when Mrs. Weiss was done, the Knitwits leaned back in their chairs, glancing at one another.

June, who was small with straight, dark gray hair, spoke first. She had a husky, determined voice, which she probably needed to be a field nurse. "Katani, we would be delighted to help you out. Wouldn't we, ladies? Everyone needs a little help in a pinch. We'll finish the scarves for you if you bring us a model and the yarn right away."

"Really? I can't believe it. I brought all the yarn. And here's a model." Smiling gratefully, Katani showed them the pink mohair scarf she'd worn over.

"Lovely, and the design looks simple enough," Sally commented. "May I take a look?"

Katani handed her the model scarf. She just couldn't believe it: They were really going to knit the scarves for her! It was a miracle! It was going to get done. Somebody was watching out for her!

"And you could do one thing for us," Frances added in a way that reminded Katani of Ms. Rodriguez. It seemed like all the best teachers had a certain way of talking, friendly but firm.

"Anything." Katani nodded.

"Deliver some scarves we already knitted to a downtown homeless shelter for women."

"The bags are right over here." Graceful, willowy Delilah rose up, standing on her toes to point out a half a dozen shopping bags lined up against the wall behind them.

"I could do that." Katani looked at Maeve. "With a little help."

"I'll help for sure," Maeve said. "We can do it. And do you think Kelley could help too?" she asked, looking at Katani.

Katani could have hugged her thoughtful friend. It was the perfect way to make Kelley feel included! "Definitely," Katani agreed.

The girls promised they would pick up the shopping bags the next afternoon to take to the homeless shelter, and then they thanked the Knitwits and waved good-bye. Outside, a thin blanket of white covered everything and the light snow was still coming down. Katani leaped into the air, throwing her arms around Mrs. Weiss and then Maeve.

"Is this really Katani Summers?" Maeve asked, smiling at her usually reserved friend.

"You saved my life!" Katani exclaimed.

Mrs. Weiss patted her on the arm and said, "That's what friends are for, dear."

15

Game On

Everybody dance now!" the voice over the huge speakers boomed, while random images of the cheering crowd flashed onto the giant scoreboard hanging from the center of the ceiling.

Isabel, Charlotte, Maeve, and Mrs. Madden were at the exhibition game to cheer Avery on, and they were having a blast! Isabel and Maeve were singing along with the rest of the crowd as fans around the arena grooved to the thumping dance beat.

"Let's dance, Isabel! Maybe we'll be up on the big screen!" Maeve shouted.

Isabel joined in as Maeve showed off her hip-hop moves, swinging and sliding side to side.

"You, too, Charlotte!" Maeve grabbed Charlotte's hand and pulled her to her feet. Charlotte smiled and shook her hips as she tried to keep up with Isabel and Maeve. They were both awesome dancers, but Charlotte liked to let loose and move to the music too—even if she wasn't the greatest dancer in the world. Mrs. Madden joined in also, clapping and dancing before leaving for the concession stand to buy snacks for everyone.

The three girls giggled as they watched a fan with zero rhythm do the twist on the scoreboard. Charlotte was secretly relieved that she wasn't that bad.

"I wish Katani could be here," Charlotte said, and sighed, still swaying her arms and hips.

"She's having a super-stressed-out week," Maeve confided, then bit her tongue to keep from saying anything about her fight with Katani or the secret of the Knitwits.

Maeve couldn't figure out a way to tell them that actually things were getting better for Katani without revealing how she'd helped Katani with the scarves.

Finally Isabel asked, "Do you guys think Katani took on too much? I mean, do you think she was too ambitious, even for the Kgirl?" Isabel kept seeing an image of her friend with a great pair of wings flying too close to the sun, like Icarus.

"I wondered about that," Charlotte said. "I heard she and Math Boy got in some kind of argument over their math project too. That doesn't sound like our Katani. I hope she doesn't do what Anne of Green Gables did—stop talking to everyone she gets in a fight with. I haven't talked to her in so long, I sort of feel like she might even be mad at me." She glanced at Isabel and hoped what she said was okay. Trying to figure out what to say and what not to say was too confusing sometimes. "Have you talked to her, Maeve?"

Maeve nodded. She was bursting to tell all about the Knitwits, the scarf project, and how Ethel Weiss had totally saved the day. But all she said was, "We talked. I went over there last night."

"You know, I think she just needed a little help, that's all," Maeve went on. She didn't think Katani would mind her saying that much. And she had to let out something or she was going to pop!

"*Katani* needed help?" Charlotte asked.

Isabel thought Maeve seemed a little smug when she replied, "Well, she's got a *lot* on her plate right now. Believe me!"

"Something *else* we don't know about?" Isabel asked pointedly.

"Oh, just everything with school and the contest!" Maeve explained quickly, putting on her most reassuring grin and shrugging (she hoped) innocently. "I'm sure Katani will tell you herself. It's almost halftime and we have to keep dancing if we're going to get up on that scoreboard. So move it, BSG! Lift those legs!" Maeve commanded her friends.

To Maeve's relief, Isabel gave herself over to the music and excitement, dancing and singing with Maeve and Charlotte and not asking any more questions about Katani. *That was close*, thought Maeve. *This keeping secrets stuff is wicked hard!*

Showtime

Avery knelt down to check her shoelaces for, like, the fiftieth time. Playing on a real NBA arena court in front of eighteen thousand fans was an earth-shattering experience. Well, maybe not eighteen thousand, since some of them would be in the bathroom or at the concession stand or whatever. In any case, there were tons of people here. She looked up to the balcony, searching for her mom and her friends, but she couldn't find them anywhere in the crowd. She hoped they could see her.

"Okay, Abigail Adams, bring it in!" Coach Porter called out, waving the five girls to gather around.

Avery's stomach was doing flips as she joined Amanda,

Sarah, Anna, and Julie in the huddle for Coach's pregame pep talk. Avery didn't usually get nervous, but playing in front of this many people was kind of intimidating. Never mind all the people watching on TV. She had to concentrate on the game. If only she could see her mother and friends in the stands, she'd feel so much better!

"Remember, girls, play together, win together, and have fun together!" Coach Porter shouted over the dance music blasting through the arena. "Go team, on three! One, two, three—"

"GO TEAM!" Avery yelled with her teammates.

As the five girls ran out on the court to warm up, Avery couldn't help but gaze up at the roof of the arena. Sixteen green and white NBA championship banners were hanging from the rafters next to the retired numbers of past Celtics stars. In the middle of the ceiling the giant cube of scoreboard flashed in time with "Everybody Dance Now!", showing fans dancing along with the music.

A girl with red hair flying was dancing like crazy and smiling right at the camera. Avery did a double-take when she realized it was Maeve! When the camera panned over, Avery saw Isabel and Charlotte dancing at Maeve's side. Even her mom was jumping up and down, pumping her arms. Avery was psyched! This was just what she needed to give her a power-boost on the court.

"Heads up, Madden!"

Avery looked to the left just as Anna whipped the ball at her. It was Avery's turn to go in for the basket. *Whoa*, she said to herself, *time to concentrate on basketball.*

Up in the stand, Mrs. Madden was squeezing her hands so tightly, her knuckles turned white. Her face looked pinched as she sucked in her breath.

"Bummer!" Isabel shouted. Avery had missed—the ball teetered on the rim and then rolled into the Palmer players' waiting hands. The other team dribbled down the court at full speed and managed a quick one-two pass. Palmer was up two points.

We have to win. Have to, have to, Avery was telling herself. She faked right and passed to the left, right on target to Anna, who lined up her shot and scored. Now she was in the zone. It was just like she'd imagined—her dream come true. The crowd had even done the wave. Avery didn't have time to look at the clock. All she thought was: two points, two points fast. Push the ball up-court!

Avery snatched up the ball and power dribbled halfway down the court and was just about to pass to Anna when the buzzer rang. It was over, the end, *finis.* Way too quick! Avery wanted to fall down and cry right there on the Celtics' court. This was not how it was supposed to end.

Coach Porter jogged up to the girls and hugged them. "Well done! Great game!"

"But we blew it!" Anna voiced Avery's own feelings.

"No way," Coach replied right away. She made all the girls face her as they headed to the locker room. "You played your hearts out. It was a short scrimmage. In a real game you would have come back, but that's not the point. You all did your best. And great job, Madden. That was a weird break in the beginning, your first shot, but you kept hammering away. You didn't give up. That's the winning ticket . . . never give up!"

Avery felt her chest fill and her spirits rise as they went into the locker room.

"One last thing," Coach Porter said to the team. "When

you go home tonight, I want you to keep one thing in mind. You all made me proud tonight, okay? It was an awesome game."

Avery's Blog:

The fans, the lights, the excitement—I mean, we're talking playing on the Celts court! It's 8–6. All I want to do is get a basket and tie up the game fast because we have to win. There I am charging down the court, sure no one is going to stop me from getting 2 points for Abigail when the buzzer goes off! JUST LIKE THAT, TIME'S UP!

Here is my question of the night: Can you be happy after you lose? Let me know what you think!

CHAPTER
16

Helping Hands

Katani was really disappointed that she had to miss Avery's exhibition game, but she had so much to do:

K*girl*™

To Do:

1. Finish lab work.

2. Write an outline for paper on Let the Circle Be Unbroken.

3. Fill out T-Biz! contest application.

4. Finalize budget and financial plans.

5. Read business articles from Mr. Sherman.

Katani felt like a spinning top. She couldn't concentrate on finishing one thing on her list because she kept thinking of all the other things she had to do. "Thank goodness for the Knitwits," she said, and sighed. But even with help from the ladies of Bluebell House, she didn't know how she could possibly finish everything on time.

Katani went to the kitchen to make a cup of tea. As she filled the kettle, she heard a sound behind her and turned around to see her mother, still in her work clothes, standing at the kitchen door. "Hey, honey," Mrs. Summers said absently, flipping through her black leather planner. "Did you finish your homework?"

That was it. First Maeve, now her mother. Katani dropped the half-full kettle in the sink and threw her arms around her mother, hot tears pouring down her face.

"Hey, what's all this for?" her mother asked, stroking her back. "Tell me what the matter is. That's what I'm here for."

Katani confessed the whole sorry story of the contest and schoolwork, Pony Camp, Reggie, Maeve, and everything. "And now time's up, and I haven't finished anything!"

Mrs. Summers clicked her PDA shut and said, "Honey, my evening is yours. We'll get whatever we need to get done for tomorrow first and then go from there. Don't you worry now. When I get in situations like this at work, I bring in the troops to help. So, let's get cracking here."

"You do?"

"Oh yes, but first I start with tea." Her mother smiled.

"Okay, thanks, Mom." Katani dried her eyes. "Lemon Lift, Cinnamon, Chai, or Earl Gray?"

"How about I'll make the tea while you bring all of your homework down here so we can get started."

"Thanks, Mom!" a grateful Katani sniffled.

"Listen, Katani." She held Katani by the shoulders. "You just have to talk to me before things get so out of control. I may be busy, but I'm always here, and so is your dad."

"I know . . . I just thought, I mean, I really thought I could do everything by myself."

"Honey," Mrs. Summers said as she turned to fill her cup with water, "it takes a village."

As she ran to get her assignment book, Katani thought about her mother's favorite quote. She had a great family and the best friends in the world, all of whom would help her anytime she asked. What had she been thinking? She had her village.

At the kitchen table, her mom typed her lab notes while Katani finished the calculations. Her lab report might not be perfect, but at least it wouldn't be late. She leaned over and gave her mother a hug. "Team Katani and Mom save the day," she whispered in her mom's ear.

"You know, Katani . . ." Mrs. Summers looked up. "You help a lot of people—Kelley, your friends, me. It's nice for us to help you back once in a while. Let it work both ways."

"I just got it set in my head to do everything myself. And I wanted to surprise you guys about the contest."

"I understand." Her mother smiled. "But, look here. We're getting there."

"Just a half hour to go," Katani said.

"I was thinking that I could swing by and pick up the Pony Camp forms on my way to or from work tomorrow."

"I guess I should have called and asked them to send them right after I realized I forgot them."

"Never mind, honey. With this workload, you can't think of everything. We'll get them, and I bet there will be space for you and Kelley. Spaces don't fill up *that* fast. Besides, everyone is so pleased with Kelley's progress, and you know how Claudia has raved about your ability and your way with horses," Mrs. Summers added.

Katani looked down.

"What is it?" her mother asked.

Katani shrugged. What she was feeling was kind of hard for her to admit, but now she knew she could tell her mom anything. "Mom, I guess I just feel lucky to have so many people helping me." She wiped a tear from the center of her eye, wondering if she should tell her mom about the Knitwits.

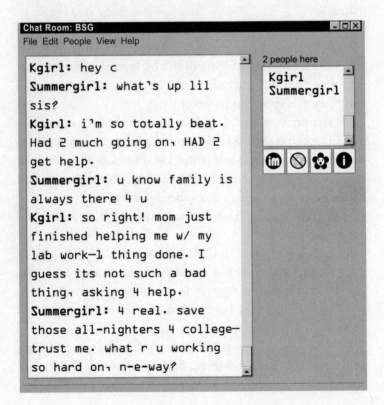

Chat Room: BSG

File Edit People View Help

2 people here

Kgirl
Summergirl

Kgirl: hey c
Summergirl: what's up lil sis?
Kgirl: i'm so totally beat. Had 2 much going on, HAD 2 get help.
Summergirl: u know family is always there 4 u
Kgirl: so right! mom just finished helping me w/ my lab work—1 thing done. I guess its not such a bad thing, asking 4 help.
Summergirl: 4 real. save those all-nighters 4 college—trust me. what r u working so hard on, n-e-way?

Kgirl: i didn't want to tell you guys at first, but im applying 4 a contest, which is due Sat.

Summergirl: u didn't want to tell?

Kgirl: i wanted it 2 b a surprise—when i won—but it was more work than i thought. i told mom everything, which is why she was helping me. will tell u the whole story, 2. have 2 sleeeeeep now. just wanted 2 say i miss u tons.

Summergirl: I miss u 2, lil sis! Don't stress. the Kgirl can do it.

2 people here

Kgirl
Summergirl

Yours Truly

"So, what's the real deal with Katani?" Avery asked as the BSG tumbled into Montoya's. "Has she transferred to another school, or what?"

"Katani who?" Isabel joked.

"She's MIA," Avery said.

"I guess she just has way too much going on this week with all this homework and the contest," Charlotte explained.

Maeve knew she couldn't keep Katani's secret for much

longer. And, really, she didn't want to. Keeping secrets from the rest of their friends was totally not BSG-style. Even Katani couldn't argue with that.

"Maeve, what aren't you telling us?" Charlotte asked.

"Do you know something we don't? You better spill," Avery told her.

"Well, Katani has things under control now . . ." Maeve paused dramatically, pretending to buff her nails. "Thanks to yours truly! I was supposed to be at a homeless shelter with Katani right now, dropping off scarves for the Knitwits, but Mrs. Fields is taking her and Kelley."

"Whoa, whoa, back up!" Avery demanded.

"*Nitwits?*" Isabel asked.

"With a K. They knit."

"Maeve, can you *please* start at the beginning?" Charlotte pleaded.

Maeve took a long sip of her hot chocolate and told the whole story of the contest, the scarves, Reggie, and especially how she, Super-Maeve, swooped in with Mrs. Weiss and the Knitwits to save the day. It felt so good to share her secret she also confessed about hiring Betsy to help her. So of course Avery, Isabel, and Charlotte had to confess they already knew. Charlotte smiled at Maeve. She knew how hard school was for Maeve.

"If Katani is okay then I am too."

Isabel nodded in agreement and raised her mug. "I propose a toast—to Maeve. Cheers!"

The girls clinked their nearly finished hot chocolates together again.

When the laughter died down, Maeve pronounced, "Topic change! I need an E News update: What's the latest on your date with Nick, Char?" Maeve asked.

Charlotte discreetly glanced around the café.

"Get real, Maeve. It's not a *date*, is it, Char?" Avery asked.

Charlotte turned red as a beet and answered, "No." She stared into her empty chocolate mug.

Maeve giggled. "Are you sure about that?"

Charlotte's Journal

Fri. night, 8:15 pm
Update: Nick and I are going to the Omni tomorrow, like we originally planned, because we both got our book reports finished. So the date—or whatever it is—is back on, I guess. I mean, what really is a date, anyway?

17

Mr. Bear Steps Out

Thanks for driving us, Grandma Ruby," Katani said. They had just picked up the scarves from the Knitwits and were on their way to deliver them to the homeless shelter downtown.

"I'm glad to do it," she answered. "Next time, my dear—"

"I know," Katani said. "Don't be afraid to ask for help!"

She was waiting for her grandmother to ask whether her schoolwork had suffered this week, but thankfully Mrs. Fields avoided that topic.

Kelley, on the other hand, was singing loudly, "We're going on a bear hunt. We're gonna catch a big one."

All afternoon Kelley had been smiling as she hugged a bright green zipped-up bag to her chest. She wouldn't let anyone else near it. Mrs. Fields already asked what was in it and got no answer, so now Katani tried.

"Do you have something special in your bag, Kelley?"

"Yes, I do. I have my own pinkie-swear secret. But I can't tell you what it is."

"A pinkie swear. I think we've had enough pinkie-swear secrets this week." Mrs. Fields looked over at Katani, who didn't even want to think about what Kelley had in there. She had enough to worry about as it was.

"We'll never find a spot for the Triple B around here," Mrs. Fields said, shaking her head at the downtown traffic and narrow streets. "So we'll use this parking garage. The shelter's just a couple blocks away."

The girls each carried two bags. Mrs. Fields rang the security bell and then spoke through the intercom, "We have a delivery from the Knitwits."

The door buzzed open, and the three of them walked into a cheery reception area. Beyond the front desk Katani saw a roomful of women and children. Many of the women were chatting and watching TV, while others looked like they were helping kids with homework or art projects. The area was buzzing with occasional laughter and the low murmur of conversation. This place was the opposite of what Katani expected when she thought of a homeless shelter.

Her grandmother opened a few of the bags to show the receptionist what they'd brought. The receptionist wrapped a purple wool scarf around her neck to model it for a few of the women walking by.

"Look at you, all dressed up and no place to go!" a pretty woman told the receptionist, and everyone laughed.

"Did you girls bring all this for us?" another woman asked, peeking into one of the bags.

"Yes, we certainly did," a stone-faced Kelley volunteered as she clutched Mr. Bear tightly. The woman stared at Kelley for a moment. Katani knew she was wondering if there was something wrong with her sister.

But all the lady said was, "Thanks very much. My

daughter needs a new scarf this year. It's a cold winter out there. Brrr!" She pulled out a cuddly looking blue one and walked away with the other women, showing it off. Katani was relieved. It was tricky with Kelley, sometimes. You just never knew how things would go.

Then suddenly, Katani had an idea. She wanted to make clothes for women like these who really needed them. Kgirl wasn't just going to be a business. Katani could design clothes that would be fashionable but still affordable and practical for real people. And when Kgirl took off, women in places like these could work on some of her projects. She could help train women too, so they could run their own businesses. She was so excited that she made a mental note to write down her ideas as soon as she got home.

Back in the car after their delivery, Katani was feeling nervous about the time. "It's getting late. The Knitwits are going to need a snack," Mrs. Fields said as she turned the car onto a busy Boylston Street. "I'll call and see if they want us to pick up some pizza."

Katani moaned. "Grandma, do we have to? It's already taking us forever to get there."

"Of course we do," Mrs. Fields replied. "If someone does something for you, you need to return the favor. Simple as that. We'll bring an early supper. Besides, if we skip eating, we'll all run out of steam before the scarves are finished."

Katani knew her grandmother was right, but the prospect of one more delay was so frustrating. All she wanted to do was get there and finish her scarves.

Mrs. Fields called Bluebell House on her cell to say she was going to stop for pizza and ask if there was a favorite topping, or a topping they couldn't eat. When she got off the phone she said, "We'll order two pies from Pizza Palace. One regular and one with soy cheese, for Natasha. It turns out she's a vegan," Mrs. Fields explained.

"What's a vegan?" Kelley asked.

"That's someone who doesn't eat anything that comes from animals, like meat or cheese or eggs, dear," Mrs. Fields explained.

"Oh," said Kelley, sitting back in her seat and looking thoughtful.

Mrs. Fields dropped the girls off with the pizza at Bluebell House, and then she drove around the corner to park the Triple B. Frances opened the door and warmly welcomed Katani and Kelley. Inside, Katani busily scanned the room for her scarves. When she saw them spread over the piano like a sea of pink, she almost felt like her old self again.

When Mrs. Fields walked in a few minutes later, Francis cried, "Why, Ruby Fields!"

"Frances Coulson!"

"What a small world!" Frances embraced Ruby. "I kept meaning to call or e-mail you after the New England Teachers Conference."

"Me too! I'm so glad to see you." Mrs. Fields shook her head. "Just because you're teaching in Somerville, that's no excuse for us not to get together."

"It took Katani's scarves for us to meet!" Frances exclaimed, and the women laughed.

Kelley sat down in a navy blue rocking chair and rocked back and forth, her head tilted up to the pale blue ceiling. Katani couldn't believe it. Here Kelley was in a strange place with all these new people and she was as calm as could be!

"We ordered a pesto and broccoli pizza because Natasha is a vegan," Kelley explained. "That means no cheeseburgers, hot dogs, milk shakes, yogurt tubes, Oreo ice cream, chicken nuggets, or fried shrimp ever!" she announced. Katani shook her head. Kelley was obviously intrigued with the vegan thing. She hoped her sister didn't go on and on about it all night.

"Well said, Kelley!" June agreed loudly. "Pizza lovers of all stripes, grab some breadsticks! A little snack will be good knitting fuel, I think. Just be careful not to spoil your dinners." When everyone had a few bites of the crunchy bread in their bellies, June ordered, "All right, knitters, pick up your needles. We're on a mission here."

Natasha gave Kelley and Mrs. Fields needles and yarn, and the Knitwits focused on their knitting. Katani had never seen people knit so quickly. It was like the Knitwits were on fast-forward. Katani settled into a big comfortable blue armchair and began adding her signature bead motif to the finished scarves. Delilah put a record on an old-fashioned record player. Then, in a sophisticated falsetto, she sang out to every single Gershwin song. Her voice was like honey—soft and smooth. *Maeve would be twirling in circles if she were here right now*, thought Katani. *That woman can sing!*

Mrs. Fields asked, "'I Got Rhythm'? I just love that song."

"I've got rhythm in my toes just listening to Delilah sing it," Frances said kindly. "We're lucky to have this songbird around the house."

"Delilah is a pretty bird!" Kelley repeated, laughing loudly.

Everyone looked up at Kelley, who had propped Mr. Bear on her lap. Now that she had everyone's attention, Kelley dramatically unzipped her green bag and pulled out a miniature version of one of Katani's scarves. Wrapping the little pink scarf around Mr. Bear's neck, she announced, "Starring

Mr. Bear—clothes by Kelley Summers, Esquire! See?"

"Why, that's about the cutest thing I've ever seen," Delilah oohed and ahhed.

"So adorable," Frances added.

"Smashing, just smashing," June pronounced.

As the Knitwits went on praising Kelley, Katani squeezed her hands into fists and counted to ten. Usually she could deal with Kelley being a distraction, but tonight she needed to get *her* scarves finished . . . pronto. To calm herself down she imagined how the store window at Think Pink! would look tomorrow with all her scarves displayed. Scarves gently folded over one another, scarves draped over fuzzy sweaters . . . wait! Maybe there was a way to include Kelley after all!

"Kelley, that's a fabulous idea," Katani exclaimed.

Mrs. Fields sent Katani the warning look, arched eyebrows and all. Katani ignored the skepticism written all over her grandmother's face and plunged on. "We can make teddy bear–size scarves just like my people-size ones and bring them to Think Pink! for the fund-raiser. I bet people would buy them for dogs to wear too. They'd look so cute in the window display next to mine, and Ms. Pink loves pets. The matching scarf theme could be part of my project—"

Kelley jumped up, clapped her hands, and threw her arms around Katani. "I'll get to meet five hundred fortunate people in D.C., too!"

"You just might," Mrs. Fields said to Kelley, laughing. She didn't say anything to Katani, but the warm smile on her face told Katani that she was definitely doing the right thing. Well, that settled it. *Sisters are way more important than prizes, anyway,* Katani thought with a smile. There would be more contests out there, but there was only one Kelley. Maybe business owners didn't have to win contests to be really successful anyway. Katani felt happy, really happy, for the first in what seemed like a very long time.

Natasha arranged the women like a factory line to incorporate Kelley's bear-size clothes into the knitting project. Incredibly organized, Natasha had the knitting system down to a science within minutes, giving each Knitwit a designated job.

"Let's rock it, ladies!" June demanded. "You think that's funny?" She pointed at Katani, who had put her hand over her mouth. Envisioning the gray-haired June "rocking" was just too much.

As they all got closer to finishing, Sally couldn't sit still. She was a first-rate Speedy Gonzales knitter, but she kept getting up to go into the kitchen. First she brought out circles of French bread with olive tapenade and roasted peppers, then marinated artichoke hearts and asparagus spears, and after that stuffed shrimp.

"These are fabulous. What's that herb?" Mrs. Fields asked.

"Marjoram," Sally said.

"Amazing. Sally, you're spoiling us!" Mrs. Fields took another shrimp. "Does she always feed you like this?"

"Oh, yes. She's trying to keep us fattened up," Delilah joked as she came in with warm pizza on a tray. At the sight of pizza, needles stopped and everyone jumped up to grab a slice.

The ladies listened respectfully as Katani filled them in on the details of the contest. Katani felt like a real professional fielding all the questions.

"Would you do anything differently?" June asked Katani while looking over at Mrs. Fields.

Katani sat back in her chair and put her paper plate down on the coffee table. She looked around at her knitting team, the women who had come to her rescue, and said, "I would ask for help at the beginning. You know, get ideas from people on the best way to do things . . . then I would get all my ducks in order. . . ."

"Quack, quack," Kelley said as she wrapped a little pink scarf around Mr. Bear's neck. June looked at Delilah, who bit her lip and raised an eyebrow at Sally, who stifled a giggle.

It was too much for Katani, who let out her first belly laugh of the week. "Kelley, you crack me up! Or should I say 'quack' me up."

Kelley looked away and began knitting another scarf.

After the pizza, Sally carried around a plate of chocolate-fudge brownies to keep everyone's energy up, she said. They were so awesome that Katani asked her for the recipe so she could make them at the next Tower sleepover. When she heard that there was puréed spinach in them, she almost fell over. Maeve collected brownie recipes, Charlotte was a true choco-holic, and Avery loved healthy food, but spinach brownies . . . the BSG would be so surprised when they tasted them!

When Kelley heard there was spinach in the brownies, she refused to believe it and would not calm down until Katani told Kelley that they were special vegan brownies. Mrs. Fields's grateful kiss on the cheek made Katani realize that managing Kelley was hard for everyone, not just her.

"Did you have enough to eat?" Sally asked everyone. "Do you need another drink?"

"If I eat anything else, somebody's going to have to carry me out," Mrs. Fields teased.

As the women continued to knit and Delilah played records, the scarves began to multiply as if by magic. Frances was like a knitting prodigy. She whirled out the most amazing patterns.

As Katani looked on, Frances explained to her the knitting and purling techniques she used to achieve different textures. Katani was thrilled to be learning so much. She settled into her chair, feeling right at home. Kelley was busy knitting tiny scarves for the fund-raiser. When the Knitwits said they couldn't believe Kelley had just started knitting, Kelley announced that she was "a Knitwit too." Katani felt a warm happiness for her sister. Kelley didn't often get compliments on her achievements.

Just before the final push, Kelley decided to count the scarves. She stopped next to her grandmother. "What is this?" Kelley held up the lopsided scarf, full of holes.

"Oh, it's fine," Frances said. "It just needs a little, um, straightening."

"Just a tad more work and it'll be fine," Delilah and Natasha agreed.

"Fine?" June asked. "It looks like moths have eaten through it."

"Poor Grandma Ruby," Kelley said sadly. "Maybe you should read Katani's knitting book."

They all laughed, including Mrs. Fields. Kelley, who wasn't really sure what was so funny, just shook her head at her grandmother.

"Another brownie, Ruby?" Sally offered.

"Oh, a small piece, I guess," Ruby answered. "It's my consolation prize."

Katani tucked away the scarf her grandmother had knitted, separating it from the pile for Think Pink! She secretly decided to bead her grandmother's scarf into something beautiful to give Mrs. Weiss as a thank-you for introducing her to her rescuers, the Knitwits.

As she looked around the blue room, all of a sudden

Katani realized the anxiety that had been plaguing her for days was completely gone. Her scarves would be finished in time! Even better, being here with the Knitwits was just like being with the BSG—an excuse to hang out and have a good time together.

"Almost there," June announced, looking at her watch.

Kelley stood up and, clutching Mr. Bear, pronounced in a loud voice, "Time's up, ladies!" Katani looked around. *Would the ladies think her sister was being rude?*

But there were chuckles all around before June answered in a softer voice than Katani had heard her use, "We'll have you over again real soon, Kelley, but I don't think we'll be knitting fourteen scarves next week."

Katani smiled at Kelley. Neither of them wanted the night to end. When it was time to leave, the normally reserved Katani gave each Knitwit a big hug and a thank-you, and promised that she would visit soon.

CHAPTER
18

With a Little Help from My Friends

On Saturday morning Katani woke to a delicious smell of coffee, cinnamon toast, eggs, and bacon. Ray Charles was on the stereo. That meant her grandmother was up and about. Ray Charles was her grandmother's favorite Saturday morning music, and "Georgia on My Mind" was one of her favorite songs in the world. It was a happy morning. Katani hugged herself. The scarves were done and life was good.

Still in her teddy bear pajamas, Kelley was at Katani's desk and counting scarves for about the hundredth time. "Twenty," she announced. "Twenty of yours and twenty of Mr. Bear's."

Isabel's older sister Elena Maria had dropped off Mrs. Martinez's three scarves last night. Katani would have to call today to thank her. She smiled and got out of bed. She usually laid out her carefully chosen outfits the night before, but the night before, Katani had been so exhausted that she fell right asleep. This morning, she grabbed a pair of jeans and a black turtleneck. "There's still a lot to do." She hugged Kelley. "But I'm starving. Aren't you?"

"Yes." Kelley's face turned serious. "You know, Katani, I like vegans, but I love pepperoni, too!"

"Me too," Katani said. "Let's go get some eggs and toast."

When they got downstairs, Mrs. Fields was sprinkling cinnamon sugar on buttered toast. Katani's dad was pouring cups of coffee, and her mother was setting plates and glasses of juice on the table.

"I heard it went well last night," Mrs. Summers said, smiling.

"It was beyond great, Mom. We finished the scarves—all fourteen I had left to do—and made scarves for teddy bears, too. That was Kelley-the-knitting-genius's idea. They'll be at the fund-raiser too—on display side by side."

Mrs. Summers pulled Katani tightly to her. "I'm proud of both my girls," she said. "Better sit down and eat. We have a big day ahead of us."

When they sat down at the breakfast table, Mr. Summers asked Katani, "So, boss, what's the game plan?"

Before she'd gone to bed, Katani had made a list of everything she had to do to get the application off today and prepare for the Think Pink! fund-raiser. As they ate, Katani went over the plan with her family. Katani couldn't believe that even Patrice was giving up her Saturday morning to help with the contest project.

"You know, I really appreciate all of your help," Katani told her family. "What would I do without my best fam?" She snapped her fingers in the air.

"We *want* to help you, Katani. That's what we're here for," her dad spoke slowly. He took a long sip of coffee. "I remember my dad saying the same thing to me once a long time ago. When I was fourteen. I had this job painting houses for the summer. I was pretty good at it too. One of the guys was afraid of heights, so he'd send me up to the top of the house. I always got stuck painting the roof trim." He shook his head and drank more coffee.

"Anyway, at the end of the summer a neighbor made me an offer. He said if I painted his whole house in a week, he'd give me two hundred dollars. I know that doesn't sound like much now, but it was a lot then, as much as I made practically all summer. If I didn't finish, I'd get nothing." He bit into a piece of bacon and chewed thoughtfully.

"It wasn't a big house but it wasn't small, either. I said yes even though I had a paper route going and school was starting that very week." He looked up at Katani. "Do you know how long it takes to paint a house?"

Katani shook her head.

"A long time. I ruined my school clothes and had to skip the first days of school." He chuckled. "I wasn't even close to finishing, but I wanted that money more than anything. Of course Dad caught me. I broke down and told him about the job. I was sure he'd make me quit right there and yell at me. Dad was kind of a yeller back then. But, instead, my father said to my brothers, 'Tomorrow we're all going over to that house and we'll stay until it's painted.'"

Mr. Summers's eyes circled his family. "That's what we're going to do today."

"Dad, we can't paint a house today. We have to finish the contest!" a worried Kelley blurted out. "Time's up, you know."

No one laughed, as they all knew Kelley hadn't meant to be funny. They could hear the urgency in her voice.

"No, we won't paint any houses today," Mr. Summers said. "We'll help Katani until her project is finished."

"And me," Kelley protested.

"Of course you," Mr. Summers said as he teasingly tugged one of Kelley's pigtails.

"All right, let's do it! Let's get this application in the mail!" Mrs. Summers declared, and started clearing the table.

Grandma Ruby brought out her trusty old typewriter and plunked it on the end of the dining room table to write up a recommendation. She said that typing on the old Remington made her more creative. Mr. Summers proofed Katani's essay and business plan one final time. Then he added a new ink cartridge to the printer so Katani could print out copies. Mrs. Summers helped arrange the scarves for Patrice to pho-to-graph, and Patrice made a bunch of eight-by-ten copies of the best shots. Kelley put the Think Pink! boxes for the scarves together, counting the total boxes and the total scarves again as she spread them in a line across the dining room table.

"Still twenty of yours and twenty of Mr. Bear's!" She danced around the kitchen happily.

As each item on her list was completed, Katani checked it off. She folded the scarves so the beaded hearts showed on the top, wrapped them in tissue, and packed them in boxes to take to Think Pink! Her mother and Patrice had offered to drop them off at the store later that day.

Next, Katani called Mrs. Martinez to thank her. *"No es nada,"* she said. Isabel said that sometimes, too. It meant "it's nothing" or "no problem."

"It's a lot," Katani told her. "I never would have gotten the project done without everyone helping me. Actually, do you mind if I tell Isabel about it now?"

"Of course!" Mrs. Martinez replied. "I will get her."

A minute later, Isabel picked up the phone. "Hey Katani. What's up?"

Katani took a deep breath. Would Isabel be mad that

Katani hadn't told her about how her mom was helping?

"Izzy, I just wanted to let you know how your mom really helped me this week," Katani began. "I was trying to do too much by myself, knitting all those scarves for the contest, so your mom offered to help me by knitting a few." Isabel was silent, so Katani pressed on. "You're really lucky to have her as your mom. So . . . thanks, I guess. For letting me benefit from a little of her mom-ness too."

When Isabel didn't respond, Katani asked, "Um, Isabel? Are you mad?"

There was a sniffle on the other end of the phone. "No!" she exclaimed, but Katani could tell she was crying. "It's just . . . thanks, Katani. I know my mom is really special. And I was wondering why she was so happy this week. I think you helped her feel useful again. My mom used to be a very busy woman—'all the time busy,' my dad used to say."

Wow! First she made Kelley happy, and now Isabel's mom. Suddenly it seemed like she was doing good deeds right and left. And it was all because she was letting other people help her too!

As soon as she got off the phone with Isabel, Katani called Maeve and asked her to come over. When Maeve arrived, Katani brought her to her bedroom and handed her one of the boxes tied with pink ribbons.

"This is for you," Katani explained. "I don't know what I would have done if you hadn't introduced me to the Knitwits. You really saved me! And Sally made the best brownies in the world. I'm going to make them for the next Tower sleepover."

Maeve opened the box to find one of the gorgeous scarves Frances knitted in every shade of pink. "Oh, Katani, I love it! It's GORGEOUS! Are you sure it's an extra?"

"I'm sure." Katani nodded. "I want you to model it tomorrow at the fund-raiser."

Maeve let out a squeal. "Me, your personal model?"

"Everyone will want one when they see you wearing it."

"Dahling, that's one assignment I can handle, no problem! I better practice."

Maeve stood in front of the mirror and wound the scarf around her neck, tying it in a knot in the front. Then she flipped the scarf back so it hung down her back and strutted around the room, pretending to talk to various crowds of people, flinging the ends of the scarf this way and that. She tucked her cascades of red hair behind her ears, wrapped the scarf over the top of her head, then tied it under her chin and pranced around the room again until Katani begged her to stop, saying, "I think I've got the image."

Suddenly Katani looked at the clock. "Whoa," she said, "I have to get to the post office before it closes."

"I'll go with you," Maeve told her, "for the good-luck walk!"

Katani had already organized and paperclipped the original application, the copies, and all the attachments. Before she put it all in an envelope, she went through her checklist one final time. Then she sealed it up and announced, "I'm ready."

"I'm going too!" Kelley said.

As the trio walked to the post office, Katani held the envelope to her chest just like Kelley had held her green bag the day before. A sliver of sun shone through the mass of gray clouds.

"I can't believe it's really done!" Katani shouted.

"Done, done, done!" Kelley sang.

Today, Kelley copying her didn't even bother Katani. She

felt like she was walking on air. "I was so stressed out this week, I never thought I'd pull it all together."

"You just needed a little help," Maeve told her, "from someone like moi. I'm your good-luck fairy!"

"Mr. Bear helped too," Kelley added.

"Yes, he did," Maeve said.

"And let's not forget the Knitwits," Katani added.

"But you pulled it all together, and I just know you're going to win!" Maeve exclaimed. "I'll be your personal model when you guys travel. I bet the great Audrey Hepburn started out modeling for one of her friends!" Audrey was Maeve's favorite old-time actress.

"We're all going to Washington—all of us, and Mr. Bear!" Kelley shouted.

"Don't count your chicks before they hatch," Katani warned her sister. But she smiled when she said it. Nothing was going to make her unhappy today.

"Look, there's Miss Pierce." Maeve waved to a petite woman walking toward them with a bag of fruit in her arms. They said hello to Charlotte's landlady, who rarely left the house.

"I saw the sun peeking out, so I decided to venture out to Yuri's for some fruit," Miss Pierce told them.

"Are you a vegan, Miss Pierce?" Kelley asked earnestly.

"No." She laughed. "I'm not. But I do love fruits and vegetables, and I hear vegans are very healthy people."

"Me either," Kelley said. She had become obsessed with who was a vegan and who was not. When she heard that Patrice's friend Shante was a vegan, Kelley really wanted to go and watch her eat. But Patrice told her it wasn't polite to talk about how and what people ate.

"I just needed a little fresh air. Where are you girls off to?" Miss Pierce continued.

"To the post office." Katani held out her envelope. "I'm mailing an application to an entrepreneur contest."

"If you go by Think Pink! you'll see Katani's scarves on display, and tomorrow they're having a fund-raiser. They're selling her scarves to raise money for breast cancer research," Maeve blurted. "You could come."

"What a lovely idea. I'll certainly try to make it," Miss Pierce replied, although the girls could hear the hesitation in her voice. Miss Pierce was a very shy woman, and social gatherings sometimes made her very nervous.

"We better hurry before the post office closes!" Katani said. "Hope to see you tomorrow, Miss Pierce."

Kgirl

To Do:

1. Call Chelsea Briggs to videotape the fund-raiser.

2. Find something to wear—maybe high black boots, black skirt, and pink V-neck sweater with ribbed waist.

3. Write something to thank everyone.

4. Make a special container for Kelley's little scarves.

5. Start English paper!!

Maeve's Notes to Self:
1. *Treat self to double Swedish Fish.*
2. *Work on performance draft of R & J (call Betsy again???) and check out Leonardo's website (he is soooo cute).*
3. *Try on outfits to wear to Think Pink! party—where I'll be the MODEL!*
4. *Paint nails the same pink as Katani's scarves.*
5. *E-mail Dad.*

CHAPTER

19

Serengeti Stampede

Charlotte was all ready to go to the Museum of Science with Nick. She had on her coolest jeans, a purple turtleneck sweater, and the comfortable leather boots she'd gotten in Paris. She decided to wear her hair down instead of in braids. In her wallet, she had thirty dollars tucked away for the subway, the movie, lunch, and in case of an emergency.

She looked out her bedroom window at the bright blue sky and suddenly wished her mom were there for her. She slipped on her mother's old jean jacket. The jacket was too big and slouchy for her, but Charlotte didn't care. Wearing it made her feel close to her mother. She wished she could ask her mom if this was a date or not. Either way, though, she was sure her mom would like Nick.

Marty ran up to her, wiggling and shaking his scruffy little body. Charlotte bent over to rub between his ears. "I already took you for a walk, little dude," she told him.

He looked up at her, begging.

"Oh, you want to come with me! I wish you could go too, Marty."

He nuzzled in closer and wagged his tail. Marty loved an outing.

"Actually, on second thought, you're the big flirt with your doggie girlfriend, La Fanny. You'd definitely call this whatever-it-is a date! You better stay here."

The phone was ringing.

"Hi Charlotte. It's Nick." He sounded kind of anxious, and Charlotte immediately wondered what was wrong. Was he canceling their date . . . er . . . non-date?

"Sorry, but I had the time wrong for the show," Nick went on. "The Planetarium starts at ten thirty and Omni starts at ten o'clock."

"Can we still get there on time?" Charlotte asked. It would be totally horrible if they missed the show!

"Not if we take the T, but don't worry, we have a ride. We'll pick you up in about ten minutes, okay?"

Charlotte breathed a sigh of relief. She wasn't getting stood up after all. "Yep, see you then," she told him.

When she got off the phone she told her father what Nick had said.

"I wonder how the Montoyas will be able to leave the bakery on a Sunday morning," Mr. Ramsey pondered. "I'd take you if I didn't have this brunch."

Charlotte knew he'd planned this brunch with some other Boston University professors over a week ago. It was the only time they could all get together. She smiled and said, "That's okay, Dad. You better make some friends if we're going to stay in Brookline for a while. What article are you writing now?"

"This piece is on Boston and how it's changed over the years."

Charlotte was relieved. That meant they were staying

in Brookline and not flying off to Switzerland or something. "Can I read it, Dad?"

"Of course you can. I would have had you proof it for me before I sent it out to a couple of magazines if *you* hadn't been so busy this week."

"Thanks for reminding me. I need to have my book report proofread too. Can you help me with that?"

"You got it."

"I better look out the window for Nick."

A few minutes later, Charlotte was thrilled to see Fabiana pull up in the Montoya minivan.

"Nick's older sister is driving us!" she called to her dad. "I'll see you this afternoon—in time for Katani's fund-raiser. Don't forget Miss Pierce is going with us!"

"I didn't forget. Have fun, sweetheart."

"You, too, Dad." Charlotte kissed her dad good-bye and ran out the door into the crisp morning air.

Charlotte was grateful that Fabiana acted like she was just picking up a friend instead of like she was picking up her brother's date. The three of them talked about school and how busy they were. Charlotte asked how her leading role in *My Fair Lady* was going and Fabiana asked her about *The Sentinel*. As they were leaving Brookline to get on Storrow Drive, Fabiana put on an ABBA CD. They cruised alongside the Charles River, the sun shining on the icy top with ABBA blasting.

"You know, Charlotte, Nick knows every single line of this album," Fabiana teased.

"No way!" Nick shouted.

But he couldn't stop himself from singing along. Fabiana and Charlotte laughed.

"Well, if I do," Nick claimed, "it's only because you play it nonstop!"

They all sang along to "Take a Chance on Me." Charlotte couldn't help reading in to the lyrics about taking a chance on someone you're crazy about. But then she quickly decided she wasn't going to worry, date or non-date! She was just going to have a good time. Still, she couldn't help thinking how cute Nick looked in his Red Sox long-sleeved T-shirt and down vest.

It definitely broke the ice having Fabiana with them. When they pulled up in front of the museum, Charlotte asked her if she wanted to join them, not wanting the fun to end.

Fabiana glanced at Nick, then said politely, "Thanks, Charlotte, but the Omni shows make me too dizzy. I'd just be sitting there with my head between my knees the whole time."

Charlotte laughed and thanked her for the ride.

As she and Nick started for the museum, Nick said, "Let's hurry, I like good seats!"

Charlotte raced in with him. They ran past the gift shop and the cafeteria, past the Discovery Center with a line of baby strollers outside. When she saw the line of people waiting in front of the Omni, she asked, "Don't we get our tickets up here, Nick?"

"I already got them," Nick said. "Online."

"Oh," Charlotte answered, trying to hold back her surprise. That was so thoughtful of him. A smile spread over her face as wide as a half moon. "That's really great. Thanks."

Nick handed in his printed tickets and they walked in to *Africa: The Secret World of the Serengeti*. Once she was sitting down, Charlotte understood how Fabiana got dizzy in here. She felt like she was hanging over a mountainside looking down at all the seats below them. As soon as the movie started, though, Charlotte forgot all about her light-headedness. The scenes of the Serengeti National Park in Tanzania where she used to live were so spectacular, but it was so odd that it felt like another lifetime that she had been there.

The lush grassland before them suddenly exploded into pounding hooves, showing the annual migration of zebras and wildebeests. Nick and Charlotte jumped in their seats as tens of thousands of hooves stampeded across the plain, shaking the ground like an earthquake. The whole theater seemed to shudder with the force of the animals running. The zebras were a mass of vertical and horizontal stripes, making it difficult to see where each individual zebra began and ended.

"That's awesome," Nick whispered.

"Zebra stripes are their self-defense. They confuse their predators that way," Charlotte whispered back. She hoped she didn't sound too much like Betsy Fitzgerald. She was just so excited, she couldn't stop herself as the camera swept over the miles of grassy plains, bush, and woodland that used to be part of her own landscape.

"Did you know that something like 750,000 zebras migrate each year, and about one and a half million wildebeests?" Charlotte whispered again.

Thousands of wildebeests, which were like large antelopes with cow horns and long wispy beards, thundered across the grasslands too.

"I can't believe you actually lived there. I have to visit Africa someday," Nick whispered back. "Maybe we can go there together," he told her shyly.

Charlotte's heart skipped a beat, and she smiled at Nick.

From a sky-view, the migration looked like a river flowing across the earth. In some places the animals ran in clusters, and in others they stretched out like ribbons. Charlotte and Nick watched the swollen rivers the animals had to cross and the snapping, hissing feeding frenzy of jackals, hyenas, and crocodiles.

"Wow," Nick said in a low voice, "this is way better than those old romantic movies Maeve is always making us watch."

Charlotte nodded as the screen suddenly turned black with an ominous rain cloud that burst, flowing in thick columns. Charlotte wanted to reach out and grab Nick's hand, but instead she said, "You can't believe the smell of the earth after it pours like that. It's so . . . pungent. And it falls so hard, only the land right under the rain cloud gets wet."

Next thing Charlotte knew, the movie was over and the lights were back on. Nick didn't seem to be in any hurry to get out of the theater, so Charlotte stayed put too.

"Where exactly did you live?" Nick asked.

"Just north of the Serengeti. The south is really a dust bowl in the dry season—until it rains, and then everything turns green like magic and the most beautiful yellow flowers grow everywhere and there are these sparkling clear pools of water."

"Sounds so incredible," Nick said.

"It's really magical. I kept thinking about my friend Shadya during the movie. I'm going to e-mail her tonight. It's so hard to keep in touch."

Nick nodded. "You know what? We should plan a trip to visit her when we graduate from high school or something."

"I bet she would love to see us. She's a very nice girl."

Not wanting to be the last ones out of the theater, they finally headed out. They heard music coming from the famous Museum of Science musical stairs and bolted in that direction.

"Wildebeest mania!" Nick yelled, running up and down. Each stair chimed a different tone when he stepped on it.

"Sounds more like a hippo!" Charlotte teased, jumping from stair to stair to hear the different tones they would play. "You know, they can run as fast as humans!"

"Charlotte, you know so much, you should write a book about the Serengeti."

"Well, my dad already did."

Nick smiled. "Oh, yeah. Hey, how about this?" He bopped up and down as he rapped "Take a Chance on Me." "Is this how it goes?"

"No, like this." Charlotte tried to move her feet to the melody of the silly ABBA song while Nick rapped until they both almost collapsed, laughing.

"I'm starving," Charlotte said when she caught her breath. "Are you?"

"Big-time. Let's grab lunch."

They raced down the musical stairs, this time with Charlotte in the lead. In the cafeteria they decided on pizza, which Charlotte insisted on paying for, even though Nick took out his wallet.

"No way," she said. "You got the tickets. I'm getting this." This way it seemed more even-Steven and not so weird. Anyway, she was having way too much fun for this to be a *date*! First dates were supposed to be awkward and nerve-racking, and Charlotte felt fine. In fact, she felt fantastic. Nick made her laugh, and she could talk to him like a friend. He even liked to talk about books. The date-non-date was perfect.

As they looked out over the partly frozen Charles River with the Prudential Building on one side and the Green Line train on the other, Nick said, "You know, watching that movie makes me want to be a world adventurer." Pausing between bites of pizza, he made a flying gesture with his hand. "I mean, I could get on a plane right this minute. I feel like I was meant to travel the world."

"I know what you mean," Charlotte agreed enthusiastically.

"Well, I guess I better call Fabiana," Nick said finally, slurping down his cold drink.

"Before she comes, let's look at the Omni schedule and pick out another movie to see," Charlotte suggested, suddenly forward. Was Nick having as good a time as she was? She couldn't believe she'd gotten up the nerve to ask him on a date—oops, non-date!

"Great idea," Nick agreed.

Charlotte slowly let out her breath and brushed her sweaty palms on her pants.

20

In the Stars

As Katani walked along Beacon Street with Kelley and her grandmother toward Think Pink! she couldn't believe that it was only a little over a week ago that she'd read about the contest in *T-Biz*. She smoothed her straight black wool miniskirt and pink cashmere sweater and laughed out loud remembering how she'd thought she could do it all by herself.

"What's so funny?" Mrs. Fields asked.

Katani threw up her hands. "How could I have ever have thought I could knit twenty scarves myself on top of everything else for school and the contest? I must have been crazy!"

"Crazy, silly, Katani," Kelley hummed. She was carrying Mr. Bear inside a basket Katani had decorated with tiny pink ribbons and a sign that read SUPPORT BREAST CANCER AWARE-NESS WEEK.

"I guess I was a little quacked," Katani teased.

"You're not a duck," Kelley shouted out, and then she sang, "We're going on a bear hunt, we're gonna catch a big one. Oh, what a beautiful day." Katani looked at her grand-mother, who raised her eyebrow and gave a small shrug. Both were hoping that Kelley would be able to keep it together for the benefit.

Up ahead, Katani saw Chelsea Briggs videotaping the Think Pink! window display. "I'll meet you there, okay?" Katani asked her grandmother.

"Yes, go on!"

"Quack, quack," Kelley called after her.

Katani waved over her shoulder to her sister and ran the rest of the way. Think Pink! looked even pinker than ever with glowing pink globe lights strung around the win-dows. Ms. Pink had wrapped Katani's scarves around snow people made of big Styrofoam balls, sparkling with pink glitter. A snow person wore a sign in the center of the display that said SUPPORT BREAST CANCER AWARENESS WEEK, with the date and time of the fund-raiser. Pink glitter snowflakes floated around the snow people and carpeted the ground. There were even adorable little snow people wearing Kelley's scarves!

"It looks so pinkalicious, doesn't it?" Katani exclaimed to Chelsea.

Chelsea put her camera on pause and agreed, "It really does."

"Thanks for taping the event, Chels. I'm really grateful."

"I'm glad to. Plus, it's good practice."

"Let's go in. I have to see everything," Katani enthused. "You look so nice, by the way."

Chelsea had on a white lambswool sweater, black jeans, and funky suede boots.

"Oh, thanks." Chelsea smiled. "My mom took me shop-ping."

The girls walked inside. More glittering snowflakes hung from the pink chandeliers above them. Katani's scarves were folded in boxes lined with pink tissue paper on the most prominent table in the store. Ms. Pink came to greet them.

"Everything looks even more scrumptiously pink than usual," Katani complimented her. "What can I do to help?"

Ms. Pink held a box of ribbon-shaped sugar cookies coated with pink icing. "You could arrange these on platters. They're donated from Party Favors. Aren't they just pink cookie perfection?"

As Mrs. Fields and Kelley walked in, Kelley announced, "I want to live here!" She quoted a sign in front of an apartment complex by the expressway in Boston. "If you lived here, you'd be home already! You'd be home already . . . you'd be home already!"

"I do feel like I live here!" Ms. Pink laughed. "Now, Kelley, you can move in right behind the counter with your grandmother for today. I want you to collect donations for the mini-scarves. Doesn't your bear look adorable!"

Chelsea started shooting video again as Kelley marched over to the counter. Chelsea zoomed in on a lovely hand-woven basket supplied by a local Cancer Support Society Crafts Program. Inside there were brochures about breast cancer prevention, and tiny pink ribbon pins. Kelley set Mr. Bear, who was modeling his hat and scarf on the counter next to the craft basket.

"Did you know that Mr. Bear and I are here to save lives?" Kelley spoke out. Last night she had listened to Katani practicing the talk she was giving today.

"That's right," Ms. Pink agreed wholeheartedly. "That's what we're all here for."

Mrs. Fields gave Kelley her first donation, which Kelley plunked into the tin, clapping proudly. Ms. Pink poured cups of pink lemonade just as the Knitwits walked in with Ethel Weiss. Right behind them were Maeve and her father. Maeve looked stunning in a scoop-neck black and pink striped knit dress and Katani's scarf wrapped loosely around her neck.

"You look lovely today, Maeve!" Kelley shouted. "Mr. Bear looks pink and lovely today too." Before Maeve could respond, Kelley was out on the floor passing her tin for donations. The Knitwits were happy to oblige. As Delilah dropped ten dollars into the tin she informed Kelley that she was doing a "terrific job."

Isabel, Avery, and Mrs. Madden arrived with a dozen pink roses for Katani. Ms. Pink gave Katani a vase, and they set the beautiful flowers on the table with Katani's scarves.

"The scarves look awesome, Katani," Isabel complimented her, gently touching the soft, pink yarn.

"Yeah, so where are these Knitwits we've heard so much about?" Avery blurted.

"Avery!" Isabel whispered sharply, elbowing her clueless friend in the ribs.

"Ouch!" Avery complained. "What was that for?"

Katani was slowly piecing it together. "Wait a minute," she said. "How do you guys know about the Knitwits?"

"Well, uhh . . ." Isabel stalled, desperately trying to think of a way to cover for Maeve.

"Maeve told us," Avery interrupted bluntly, turning to check out the table with refreshments. "Hey, those cookies look awesome! Be right back," she called over her shoulder, dashing away into the crowd.

"Maeve told you?" Katani repeated, feeling a little betrayed. Katani was happy for everyone to know all about the Knitwits *now*, but back when Maeve came up with the idea, Katani hadn't wanted anyone to know she couldn't do it all on her own. Was she wrong to have trusted Maeve with her secret?

"She only told us because we were all so worried about you, Katani," Isabel explained. Katani nodded and watched Maeve modeling the scarf. Seeing her chatting away happily with the other guests, Katani instantly forgave her friend. It was just too hard to stay mad at bright, bubbly Maeve! Besides, Katani also realized that it was wrong of her to expect Maeve to keep secrets from the BSG. *From now on, no more secrets among friends . . . unless it is a surprise birthday party*, Katani promised herself.

"It's no big deal," Katani reassured Isabel with a smile. "Avery's right. Let's try those cookies!"

Katani looked up to see that Mr. Ramsey, Charlotte, and Miss Pierce had just arrived when everything suddenly went dark and she felt a pair of hand over her eyes. A familiar voice from behind her asked, "Guess who?"

Katani spun around. "Candice! You came all the way home for this?"

"I wouldn't have missed it for the world, little sis. Those scarves look so cool. No wonder you were so crazy busy!" Candice hugged Katani. "But you did it, girl!"

"With a little help from my my friends," Katani gestured to Maeve and the Knitwits.

Support for Katani and Ms. Pink kept pouring through the doors. There were friends of Ms. Pink, store regulars, owners of other nearby stores, and random people passing by the party. Ms. Rodriguez even showed up. Betsy Fitzgerald walked right up to Katani and gave her a warm congratulations, and then bought a scarf for her mother's bulldog. Katani decided to let go of her competitive feelings—at least for the time being.

Just when Katani thought there wasn't room for anyone else in the store, the mayor of Boston walked through the doors! "Katani!" Maeve squeaked in her ear. "This is your big break!" Before Katani knew it, Ms. Pink was introducing the mayor to her.

"Here's the young entrepreneur responsible for all the scarves at our fund-raiser. Mr. Mayor, Katani Summers."

Patrice took out her digital camera as Katani and the mayor shook hands. At the same time, Chelsea moved in, capturing the moment on her video camera. The mayor's assistant draped one of Katani's scarves over the mayor's arm.

"You've got quite a business going," the mayor said.

"I'm planning to create a fashion design company called Kgirl," Katani told him proudly.

"I certainly have no doubts it'll be a huge success. You've done fine work, Katooni." The mayor threw the scarf around his neck. "I'll take this one for my wife."

"Yay, Katooni!" clapped an irreverent Avery with a big grin.

Katani almost lost it watching Avery, but she managed to blurt out a "thank you." She was relieved when Patrice stepped toward them.

"Excuse me, may I take a picture, Mr. Mayor? Katooni is my younger sister," Patrice added with a mischievous grin. Katani wanted to kill her.

Side by side, Katani and the mayor smiled at Patrice, who clicked away until a swarm of people who were waiting to speak to the mayor edged in. Before he turned to them, he put his hand on Katani's arm and said, "Congratulations, a job well done." Thank goodness he did not say "Katooni" one more time. If he had, she would have completely lost it.

"Thank you very much. It was nice to meet you," Katani said, then stuck out her hand and smiled at the mayor of Boston. She watched the crowd surround him as Ms. Pink escorted him around the store.

"Wow, the mayor is wearing your scarf!" Patrice showed Katani the pictures. "Aren't they great? You should email these to *T-Biz!* for the contest."

"Don't you think it's too late?"

"No, and it could really help your chances of winning. And while you're at it, send the pictures to the *Globe*, too. Make sure you spell your name right," she said, laughing.

"All right, let's do it as soon as we get home," Katani agreed, refusing to take her sister's bait.

Patrice gave Katani a high five.

Then Candice joined them. "You rock, Kgirl!"

"I should have told the mayor what a good job *he* was doing," Katani said with sudden embarrassment.

"I always think of everything I should have said a few minutes after the fact," Candice sympathized. "If the mayor came up to me, I'd probably faint. Don't worry, you were fabulous!"

Katani pointed to Kelley. "I'm not the only star."

The mayor was now shaking hands with Mrs. Fields and Kelley. The room grew quiet for a moment, and they heard Kelley say, "This is Mr. Bear."

The mayor shook Mr. Bear's hand and congratulated Kelley for all her hard work. A few cameras snapped. Katani was proud of Kelley. After all, they *were* in this together.

Just as Katani was about to check on the scarf display, a woman with soft brown eyes and hair pulled back in a tight ponytail approached her, introducing herself as a representative from the Dana-Farber Cancer Institute.

"I just love your scarves," she said. "The beads are such a charming touch. The colors are perfect for our cause," the woman gushed. "I thought you might be interested in knitting scarves to sell on our online charity site. Like this fund-raiser, a portion of the proceeds will go to breast cancer research and treatment."

"Really?" Katani couldn't believe her ears.

"Here's my card. You can call or e-mail me at your convenience."

"Okay! Thank you so much." *This time around*, Katani resolved, *I'll consult with my new "board of advisers"—Mom, Dad, Grandma Ruby, Ms. Pink, Maeve, and Kelley—way earlier in the game.*

Charlotte, Isabel, and Avery came up and handed Katani a cup of lemonade. They toasted, "To Katani and this amazing party! You pulled it off!"

"I'm really sorry, you guys," Katani said, sipping her drink. "I feel like I haven't seen my best friends in so long, except for Maeve."

They glanced over at model Maeve standing behind the scarf table, turning side to side with her hands on her hips. The pink lights shone on her hair, making it shine a vibrant pink too.

"Look, Katani, your scarves are almost gone!" Isabel pointed to the display table where there were only a few boxes left.

The girls looked around the room, glowing pink and full of people talking, laughing, and toasting cups of lemonade. Chelsea was zooming her camera in on Mr. Ramsey and Mr. Taylor browsing through the selection of pink books, both looking kind of uncomfortable surrounded by all the pink-ness. Betsy and Ms. R were helping themselves to the pink-ribbon cookies.

"Betsy's probably talking to Ms. R about her book report," Avery quipped.

"I should be talking to her about mine," Katani replied. "I haven't even started yet!"

"I guess you've been just a tiny bit busy, Katooni," joked Avery.

"And now my time's almost up," Katani said calmly as she yanked Avery's ponytail. "But I really learned the hard way that I need to lean on people sometimes, as my mom put it. She says that's what family and friends are for." Then Katani turned to Charlotte. "I didn't even ask how your date with Nick was."

Charlotte giggled. "Well, I still have no idea if it actually was a date, but we had so much fun. We both felt like we were really in Africa." Charlotte felt her cheeks go hot when she realized Chelsea had come out of nowhere and was videotaping the BSG. She tried to hide behind her lemonade cup as the others waved to Chelsea.

"We better save this footage for the day Katani is rich and famous," Chelsea told them, "to remind her of her roots!"

They all laughed.

"Details about you-know-what later," Katani told Charlotte. "Right now I better check on how Kelley and my grandma are doing."

Katani whirled around and ran right smack into her friend Marky from High Hopes. "Marky, I'm sorry!" she exclaimed.

"That's okay." Marky laughed. "It's so crowded in here!"

"It's jammed!" Katani smiled at her friend. "I didn't know you were coming."

"I wouldn't have been able to if Whitney hadn't come over this morning to help me with my social studies project." Katani couldn't help but wonder how Whitney had time to help anyone, what with her extra riding lessons and super-successful barrette business. "I was complaining yesterday at the stable about this paper on China," Marky went on, "and she just said, 'Do you want some help? I lived in China for a year.' She totally saved me."

"Whitney did that?"

Marky nodded. "She's really nice, you know. Once you get to know her."

"Mmm-hmm." Katani couldn't take all this in right now. "I better go check in with my sis. She's collecting donations over there." Katani pointed at the counter.

"Well, congrats, Katani."

"Thanks. Oh, and thanks for coming too."

Katani hurried over to find Kelley, trying to make sense of everything in her head. On top of everything, had she been unfair to Whitney?

Sapphire Pierce was leaning on the counter across from Mrs. Fields and Kelley. "You must be so proud of your granddaughters," she told Mrs. Fields.

"I certainly am," Mrs. Fields replied with a smile.

"Katani!" Kelley shouted. "Mr. Bear's scarves are all gone, even the one he was modeling, and I shook hands with the mayor! The smiley mayor of Boston! He mumbles, you know."

"Kelley, you're a superstar! Can I please shake Ms. Kelley Summers's hand, too?" Katani leaned over the counter, extending her hand.

Kelley shook her head. "No, Katani, I am all shook out."

"That's okay, Kel," Katani said, and blew her sister a kiss.

Just then Ms. Pink flashed the store lights on and off, and the room quieted down. "Hello, everyone. For those of you who don't know me, I'm Razzberry Pink, and this is my store. I want to thank everyone for coming out today to support our fund-raiser. The power to fight cancer comes from the heart and—" She paused. "From the pocketbook."

Laughter rippled through the room.

"We all know what a pink ribbon means," Ms. Pink continued, "and as you can see by looking around you, you're in the right place. Now, I am so pleased to introduce Katani Summers, who is the girl behind these beautiful scarves. Katani, come on up and say a few words."

Kelley held up Mr. Bear and shouted, "Wooo-hooo!"

Katani stepped to the center of the room. She had prepared a short speech, but now she decided to keep her paper folded in her hand.

"Thank you, everyone, for being here today to support such a good cause," Katani spoke clearly, her eyes circling the room. "I had this idea to start a business to support a worthy cause. But this past week I was so busy with school work, an entrepreneur contest, and this fund-raiser, I somehow forgot what was most important—*working together*. I thought I could do it all myself, but I learned my lesson."

"I told you, you needed help!" Kelley blurted out.

A few people laughed, including Katani. "You were so right, Kelley," she agreed. "And now I want to thank everyone who helped me get to this point today: my friend Maeve; my entire family; Kelley, for her perfect mini-scarves; Mrs. Martinez; the Knitwits; and finally, Ms. Pink, for hosting this special party at her spectacular pink store. But, most importantly, thank you all for being here today and contributing to the Race for the Cure!"

As Katani paused, the room was so quiet, she could hear Chelsea's video camera making a low whirring noise. She glanced down at her notes to make sure she got this next part exactly right.

"Working together, we can really make a difference—no matter how old or young we are." Katani raised her lemonade cup to toast everyone. Ms. Pink threw a rain shower of sparkling pink confetti on everyone, and Maeve pronounced the event "Miraculous, simply miraculous!"

Epilogue

One Week Later

```
Chat Room: BSG                                    _ □ X
File Edit People View Help

 flikchic: can we talk book      ▲   5 people here
 reports? i have a major
 announcement 2 make 2 every1        4kicks
 who doesn't know i got a            lafrida
 B+!!!! only my best grade           skywriter
 ever!!!                             flikchic
 4kicks: u'd think a B+ was          Kgirl
 the highest grade any1 ever
 got in the history of the
 world!
 flikchic: it is—in Maeve
 history! any1 up 4 Montoya's
 2morrow?
 4kicks: i will even though      ▼
```

I got a C+. given my week,
i'll take it
Kgirl: i have 2 go c Ms. R
about my B- :)
flikchic: that must b like
ur worst grade ever
4kicks: my mom says even
super-organized people
collapse w/ an overload of
work . . . and given that
i'm not super organized,
next time she said, I'll
have 2 cut back on activi-
ties :) :) which means the
rock climbing team might be
out :(
Kgirl: i shoulda started
reading sooner. i already
made up my next 2-do list—#1
PRIORITIZE! the thing that
gets me is let the circle is
my favorite book (I've read
it like 100 x) and i know i
didn't do as good a job as I
could've
4kicks: me either w/MLK. my
mom was Disappointed w/ a
capital D. but I learned a
lot & i posted it on my blog

5 people here

4kicks
lafrida
skywriter
flikchic
Kgirl

& people said they liked
it. anyway I'm so in2 rock
climbing now
lafrida: ave, mayb next time
u should perform ur project
flikchic: gr8 idea! i can
help u. ms r loved my
costumes and the parts i
memorized and all the clips
of romeo & juliet. i think
i woulda gotten an A if my
monologues weren't so long
4kicks: you mean like
4ever!!
flikchic: we r talking r &
j! next time ms r said we
had 2 meet 2 go over the
performance 1st. whatever
skywriter: i coulda listened
4 way longer
Kgirl: me 2
lafrida: ditto maeve. u were
great
flikchic: thanks
4kicks: sorry, i sorta zoned
1/2way through thinking bout
hoops
Kgirl: LOL! what about u,
izzy and char? r u going 2

5 people here

4kicks
lafrida
skywriter
flikchic
Kgirl

tell us about urs?

lafrida: i got an A 4 "a dangerous flight."

skywriter: izzy, thats so great! what'd ms. r say?

flikchic: and y haven't we seen ur book?

lafrida: she still has it. she wants 2 show it 2 a group of teachers

Kgirl: no way, girl! y didnt u tell us?

lafrida: i guess im still kinda in shock! its the best grade i ever got outside of art class ever in my whole life. im pretty stoked. my mom and Aunt Lourdes 2

skywriter: I got an A on anne of green gables.

lafrida: YAY!

4kicks: and u finished early! u rock!

Kgirl: I have some good news too

flikchic: ooo I bet I know! is it the contest?

Kgirl: yep i got a call from T-Biz today & guess what????

5 people here

4kicks
lafrida
skywriter
flikchic
Kgirl

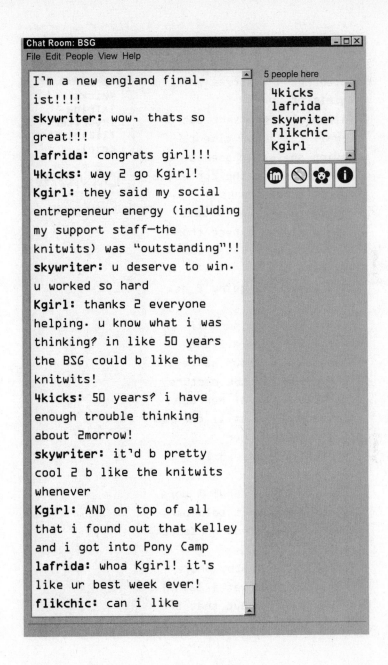

I'm a new england final-
ist!!!!
skywriter: wow, thats so
great!!!
lafrida: congrats girl!!!
4kicks: way 2 go Kgirl!
Kgirl: they said my social
entrepreneur energy (including
my support staff—the
knitwits) was "outstanding"!!
skywriter: u deserve to win.
u worked so hard
Kgirl: thanks 2 everyone
helping. u know what i was
thinking? in like 50 years
the BSG could b like the
knitwits!
4kicks: 50 years? i have
enough trouble thinking
about 2morrow!
skywriter: it'd b pretty
cool 2 b like the knitwits
whenever
Kgirl: AND on top of all
that i found out that Kelley
and i got into Pony Camp
lafrida: whoa Kgirl! it's
like ur best week ever!
flikchic: can i like

5 people here

4kicks
lafrida
skywriter
flikchic
Kgirl

File Edit People View Help

interrupt 4 a sec?

Kgirl: OK

flikchic: betsy sent out an e-mail 2 all her clients saying she was chosen as a NE finalist in the contest 2

Kgirl: hmmmm—thanks 4 letting me no . . . what else would we expect from betsy anyway?

4kicks: lol.

skywriter: r u going 2 dc, katani?

Kgirl: yes! not sure if Kelley will go. all she seems 2 care about since the fund-raiser is the picture from the globe of her and the mayor! she still carries it around with her

lafrida: she showed it 2 every1!

Kgirl: thats 4 sure! 1 more thing. remember i told u about whitney from horseback riding?

lafrida: the snobby one?

Kgirl: is that wat i said?! anyway I found out that she

5 people here

4kicks
lafrida
skywriter
flikchic
Kgirl

didn't enter the contest

skywriter: what r u going 2 do now?

Kgirl: i don't know, i think I might have made a mistake about her! I'm going to High Hopes 2morrow. i'll let you know what happens. . . .

5 people here

4kicks
lafrida
skywriter
flikchic
Kgirl

Time's Up BOOK EXTRAS

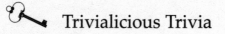
Trivialicious Trivia

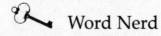
Word Nerd

Book Club Buzz

Time's Up triviαlicious triviα

1. What is Katani's favorite magazine?
   A. *Teen Business Week*
   B. *Forbes Kids*
   C. *T-Biz! A Magazine for Teen Entrepreneurs*
   D. *Teen Business: A Magazine for Teen Entrepreneurs*

2. What is the name of the climbing team Avery joins?
   A. Watertown Adventure Climbing Team
   B. Watertown Rocks!
   C. Watertown Climbers
   D. Watertown Teen Climbing Team

3. What does Whitney make and sell for her business?
   A. barrettes with painted horses
   B. wool scarves
   C. leather riding gloves
   D. barrettes with painted birds

4. What is Maevelicious Pink Pluff made of?
   A. cotton candy ice cream and chocolate sauce
   B. strawberry swirl ice cream and Marshmallow Fluff
   C. raspberry jam and vanilla Jell-O Pudding
   D. strawberry yogurt and mini-marshmallows

5. What charity event does Ms. Pink ask Katani to knit scarves for?
   A. Diabetes Awareness Week
   B. World Mental Health Day
   C. Autism Awareness Month
   D. Breast Cancer Awareness Week

6. Who is Betsy's favorite cute boy on Maeve's "crush alert" wall?
   A. Leonardo DiCaprio
   B. Daniel Radcliffe
   C. Orlando Bloom
   D. Zac Efron

7. What do the Knitwits call their home?
   A. Blueberry House
   B. Bluebell House
   C. Bluebird Bungalow
   D. Blue Sky Manor

8. Who sings Mrs. Fields's favorite Saturday morning music?
   A. George Gershwin
   B. Ray Charles
   C. Louis Armstrong
   D. Ella Fitzgerald

9. What does Katani ask Maeve to do, to thank her for all her help?
   A. model scarves at the fund-raiser
   B. DJ for the fund-raiser
   C. sell scarves at the fund-raiser
   D. dance at the fund-raiser

10. What song do Charlotte and Nick try to play on the musical stairs?
    A. "Under Pressure"
    B. "Everybody Dance Now!"
    C. "Georgia on My Mind"
    D. "Take a Chance on Me"

ANSWERS: 1. C. *T-Biz! A Magazine for Teen Entrepreneurs* 2. A. Watertown Adventure Climbing Team 3. A. Barrettes with painted horses 4. B. Strawberry swirl ice cream and Marshmallow Fluff 5. D. Breast Cancer Awareness Week 6. C. Orlando Bloom 7. B. Bluebell House 8. B. Ray Charles 9. A. Model scarves at the fund-raiser 10. D. "Take a Chance on Me"

Word Nerd

BSG Words

(name)alicious: (p. 15) adjective—*a way to describe someone so cool and sweet, you could just eat him or her up.*

major 411: (p. 61) noun—*a start-with-the-basics explanation of something.*

all-nighter: (p. 69) noun—*staying up all night to finish a project so it won't be late.*

Knitwit: (p. 124) noun—*someone who loves to knit!*

Spanish Words and Phrases

¡Vámanos!: (p. 106)—*Let's go!*

No es nada: (p. 155)—*It's nothing.*

Other Cool Words

entrepreneur: (p. 1) noun—*a person who starts and runs her own business.*

mohair: (p. 11) noun—*yarn made from Angora goat hair.*

Pegasus: (p. 23) noun—*a mythical Greek horse with big wings.*

Method acting: (p. 29) noun—*when an actor uses her own emotions and life experiences to understand a character she's playing.*

wave, the: (p. 30) noun—*when each member of a group, one after another, stands and waves their hands in the air, then sits back* *down. From a distance, it looks like a rolling wave.*

nemesis: (p. 49) noun—*an enemy you can't win against.*

purl: (p. 59) noun—*a basic stitch for knitting. A purled stitch looks like a little bump.*

archetypal: (p. 80) adjective—*an example of an idea that's so perfect, a lot of similar ideas have been based on it.*

scrimmage: (p. 88) noun—*a just-for-fun basketball game played by two five-player teams.*

bibliography: (p. 97) noun—*a list of authors or books that were used for a research project.*

Chai tea: (p. 114) noun—*black tea mixed with cardamom, and other tasty spices like cinnamon, ginger, and cloves.*

hibernation: (p. 118) noun—*the state animals like bears are in when they settle in to sleep through the winter.*

wildebeest: (p. 165) noun—*a big, horned African antelope that looks a bit like an ox. Also known as a gnu.*

pungent: (p. 166) adjective—*having a strong smell or taste.*

Book Club Buzz

10 QUESTIONS FOR YOU AND YOUR FRIENDS TO CHAT ABOUT

1. If you were going to enter an entrepreneur contest, what kind of business would you want to start?

2. Why doesn't Katani want her family to know she's entering the Entrepreneur of the Year contest? Have you ever tried to keep a secret from your family or friends? What happened?

3. Have you ever bitten off more than you could chew? How did you handle it?

4. How does each BSG use her talents and interests to turn the book report from a chore into something she can have fun with?

5. Katani asks her sister Candice for advice on what she does when she's "totally stressed." When you're feeling stressed, how do you chill out?

6. Maeve decides to ask for Betsy's help even though she knows Katani's feelings will be hurt when she finds out. Do you think she has a right to ask whomever she wants for help with her homework, or should she have talked to Katani and the BSG before calling Betsy?

7. Maeve says pink relaxes her, and Betsy finds it easier to concentrate in a room with no distractions, like Maeve's kitchen. Is there a color, or a kind of music, or something else that helps you focus on getting your work done?

8. If you were in Reggie's shoes, how would you have handled Katani forgetting to meet you after school? Would you have given her a second chance, or would you have preferred to work alone?

9. Maeve says, "When in doubt, call a BSG." Which of the girls' problems could have been avoided if they'd talked to one another and asked for help instead of keeping their problems secret?

10. Katani worries that the BSG will be mad when she finally tells them the truth about what's been going on. Would you be mad at a friend if you found out she'd been keeping a problem secret from you, or would you want to help her—or both?

What's next for the

BEACON STREET GIRLS

Green Algae and Bubblegum Wars

Science isn't exactly Maeve's favorite subject, but she's still excited to be going to the Sally Ride Science Festival at MIT with her hunky tutor, Matt. Sure, the BSG and Maeve's annoyingly brilliant younger brother are going as well, but it's still *almost* kind of a date, isn't it? And it's an opportunity for Maeve and crew to try out their match-making skills on Avery's brother, Scott, and Isabel's sister, Elena Maria.

The festival gives the BSG a super idea—an environmental science fair at Abigail Adams Junior High. Soon everyone's hard to save the planet. But plans for a bubblegum factory nearby put Avery and Katani on opposite sides of an environmental issue—and Avery finds herself in a bubblegum war with the Queens of Mean!

Check out the Beacon Street Girls at
www.beaconstreetgirls.com

Aladdin M!X

Collect all the BSG books today!

#1 Worst Enemies/Best Friends ☐ **READ IT!**
Yikes! As if being the new girl isn't bad enough ... Charlotte just made
the biggest cafeteria blunder in the history of Abigail Adams Junior High.

#2 Bad News/Good News ☐ **READ IT!**
Charlotte can't believe it. Her father wants to move away again, and
the timing couldn't be worse for the Beacon Street Girls.

#3 Letters from the Heart ☐ **READ IT!**
Life seems perfect for Maeve and Avery ... until they find out that in
seventh grade, the world can turn upside down just like that.

#4 Out of Bounds ☐ **READ IT!**
Can the Beacon Street Girls bring the house down at Abigail Adams
Junior High's Talent Show? Or will the Queens of Mean steal the show?

#5 Promises, Promises ☐ **READ IT!**
Elections for class president are underway, and the Beacon
treet Girls are right in the middle of it all. The drama escalates
when election posters start to disappear.

#6 Lake Rescue ☐ **READ IT!**
Big time fun awaits the Beacon Street Girls and the rest of the seventh
grade. The class is heading to Lake Rescue in New Hampshire for
outdoor adventure.

#7 Freaked Out ☐ **READ IT!**
The party of the year is just around the corner. What happens when
the party invitations are given out ... but not to everyone?

#8 Lucky Charm ☐ **READ IT!**
Marty is missing! The BSG begin a desperate search for their beloved
doggie mascot which leads them to an unexpected and famous
person.

#9 Fashion Frenzy

☐ **READ IT!**

Katani and Maeve head to New York City to experience a teen fashion show. They learn the hard way that fashion is all about self-expression and being true to one's self.

#10 Just Kidding

☐ **READ IT!**

Spirit Week at Abigail Adams Junior High should mean fun and excitement. But when mean emails circulate about Isabel and Kevin Connors, Spirit Week takes a turn for the worse.

#11 Ghost Town

☐ **READ IT!**

The BSG are off to a real Montana dude ranch for a fun-filled week of skiing, snowboarding, cowboys, and celebrity twins ... plus a ghost town full of secrets.

#12 Time's Up

☐ **READ IT!**

Katani knows she can win the business contest. But with school and friends and family taking up all her time, has she gotten in over her head?

Also . . . Our Special Adventure Series:

Charlotte in Paris

☐ **READ IT!**

Something mysterious happens when Charlotte returns to Paris to search for her long lost cat and to visit her best Parisian friend, Sophie.

Maeve on the Red Carpet

☐ **READ IT!**

Film camp at Maeve's own Movie House is oh-so-fabulous. But is Maeve's new friend, Madeline Von Krupcake the star of the Maddiecake commercials, really as sweet as the cakes she sells?

Freestyle with Avery

☐ **READ IT!**

Avery Madden can't wait to go to Telluride, Colorado to visit her dad! But there's one surprise that Avery's definitely not expecting.

Katani's Jamaican Holiday

☐ **READ IT!**

Katani's first Caribbean vacation is more mystery and adventure than lazy beach days, with a mysterious old lady, a lost heirloom necklace, and a competitive businessman scheming to take over the family banana bread bakery.

Charlotte
the dreamy
world traveler
who loves to write

Katani
the stylish,
brainy, and loyal
fashionista

Maeve
the effervescent
movie star
in training

Avery
the outspoken
sports and
pet lover

Isabel
the creative,
quiet, and
friendly artist

Meet the
Beacon Street Girls ...
They're real, they're fun—
they're just like you!

Once upon a time ...
There were five girls: **Charlotte, Katani,
Maeve, Avery** and **Isabel**.
One night at a sleepover they discovered
a secret tower and became best friends.
Now the **Beacon Street Girls** (BSG)
have special adventures,
and lots and lots of
super sleepovers.

www.beaconstreetgirls.com

Follow the adventures of the **Beacon Street Girls** and
their adopted mutt Marty @ www.beaconstreetgirls.com
and in our fun and friend-focused books.

BEACON STREET GIRLS

FREE!

www.BeaconStreetGirls.com

✿ Play games

✿ Meet the Beacon Street Girls

✿ Tour the Beacon Street neighborhood

✿ Read sneak peeks of upcoming books

✿ Visit the BSG online Shop

✿ Take cool quizzes

... and more!

Fun stuff for everyone!

Don't forget to visit
www.BeaconStreetGirls.com
to play our games,
meet friends & more!